PRAISE FOR *PLACES LIKE THESE*

"The stories in Lauren Carter's *Places Like These* explore the
landscape of grief and anxiety that disrupt the quietude of
so-called ordinary lives and places. Carter turns her
penetrating writer's gaze toward that which makes us human,
the ways in which we must carry on, for better and for worse.
I loved this highly readable collection."
—Nancy Jo Cullen, author of
The Western Alienation Merit Badge

"*Places Like These* by Lauren Carter offers a magnetic and
clear-eyed examination of the times in our lives when
we can say we've truly lived. Told with Carter's unmistakably
world-bending lyricism, the stories in this collection splinter
with moments of seismic recognition; they tug at the places
in ourselves we've forgotten existed but inform who we are.
An unforgettable read."
—Hollay Ghadery, author of *Fuse*

"One cannot help but stop and wonder at
the beauty of Carter's craft and skill."
—Kim Fahner

"Carter dips into some pretty dark realities,
but she does it so gently. This is just the kind of truthful,
compassionate storytelling the world needs now."
—Angeline Schellenberg

"With depth of feeling and restraint of language, [Carter]
offers us a balancing act of heritage, hardship, and hope."
—Scotiabank Giller Prize–winning author Ian Williams

"Carter's prose is not flashy, but it is clear, fresh,
and effective: the right words in the right order.
She has mastered all the necessary elements, from
characterization to pace; we feel, understand, connect."
—*Alberta Views*

lauren carter

places like these

stories

Book*hug Press
TORONTO 2023

FIRST EDITION

Library and Archives Canada Cataloguing in Publication

Title: Places like these : stories / Lauren Carter.
Names: Carter, Lauren, 1972– author.
Identifiers: Canadiana (print) 20220457506 | Canadiana (ebook)
20220457557
    ISBN 9781771668057 (softcover)
    ISBN 9781771668071 (PDF)
    ISBN 9781771668064 (EPUB)
Classification: LCC PS8605.A863 P53 2023 | DDC C813/.6—dc23

The production of this book was made possible through the generous
assistance of the Canada Council for the Arts and the Ontario Arts
Council. Book*hug Press also acknowledges the support of the Government
of Canada through the Canada Book Fund and the Government of
Ontario through the Ontario Book Publishing Tax Credit and the Ontario
Book Fund.

Book*hug Press acknowledges that the land on which we operate is
the traditional territory of many nations, including the Mississaugas
of the Credit, the Anishnabeg, the Chippewa, the Haudenosaunee,
and the Wendat peoples. We recognize the enduring presence of many
diverse First Nations, Inuit, and Métis peoples and are grateful for the
opportunity to meet, work, and learn on this territory.

*For my sister, Carey, with whom I've shared
so many places like these.*

"There isn't a story in the world that
isn't in part, at least, addressed to the past."
—Colum McCann

Contents

Bones

The butcher was out on the highway, north of town. Luke and I drove out to buy bones for Barry Allen, a plastic bag of them, but a *Closed* sign hung in the darkened window. "He's gone to deliver the pig," said the man behind the counter in the furniture liquidation store that had moved into the community building next door. "For the Hawaiian supper," he said.

All week I'd wanted to go to that. The letters on the sign-board outside the hotel dining room said *Ho'olu Komo la Kaua*, which meant *Please Join Us*, according to the internet. In the forest behind our house, the poplar leaves and tamarack needles blazed yellow against the dark green of jack pine and black spruce. It was easy to see that winter was on the way. Already the car had to be warmed up, my breath a fog in front of my face in the early morning.

It was our second autumn up north, but the year before I had missed most of the changes. For all of last October, I'd been back home, helping sort my mother's dishes, books, and odds and ends into piles labelled *Keep* and *Give Away* for her move into a condo overlooking the eighth hole of a golf course outside Gravenhurst, and appearing in court for my stepbrother's trial. My sister was home, too, all the way from Vancouver, but she didn't really speak with our stepbrother anymore, had never seen the inside of his apartment, didn't know the streets he walked, sometimes skateboarded, late at night. We are not an ordinary family, never have been, if there is such a thing.

"Twenty minutes," the furniture guy said, so Luke and I talked about whether to wait or drive back into town, drop my books off at the library, pick up the mail, buy our weekly box of cheap Riesling at the Liquor Mart. Barry Allen was back at our apartment, in a corral-like cage in the corner of the kitchen, slowly healing from his knee surgery. He had a cone on, what the vet called an Elizabethan collar, but he still managed to work the marrow out of cut lengths of bone within a couple hours. Gently, he would take them from my hand in jaws designed to grip and hold. He'd set them down on the inside of his cone, which was flattened like a plastic placemat, before unpeeling the skein of frozen skin with his front teeth, licking the hard, yellowish cap. The bones kept him busy, gave him something to do during the twelve weeks it would take for his tibia to knit together underneath the steel plate.

It had already been a month, and in the corner of his cage a pile of hollowed-out bones clattered like wind chimes whenever he spun awkwardly around, lifting his healing leg, making a place to settle.

Luke and I waited a few minutes, strolling through the crowded leather couches, television sets, stacked microwaves, and boxed table settings—the things people might buy us, I remember thinking, if we ever got married. A couple times Luke had asked me what we were waiting for, and while I hadn't been able to verbalize a clear answer, I did know that, up until we got Barry Allen, it had felt like something was missing. Some kind of stability. Some kind of day-to-day sense of being rooted, so we could settle into the enclosure of a married life and feel secure.

The butcher was taking too long, so after Luke bought a new travel mug, we decided to drive into town. On the way past the IGA in the mall, I said, "Why don't we get a chicken."

"What do you want a chicken for?"

"For supper. Duh."

He shook his head sharply, pouting. He'd been in a bad mood for a while, and I thought I knew why. We'd gotten the dog, a black pit-bull mix, to go duck hunting and camping and fishing with us. We'd saved up a lot of money to buy a motorboat and then had to spend it all, plus more from my credit card, on the surgery, with another for Barry Allen's right leg on the way. The tendon in that knee was also fraying. "They go like rope," the vet had told us at the animal hospital in Saskatoon, gesturing to the model on his desk. "Strand by strand, until only a single thread remains." He touched his fingers together, pulled them abruptly apart. "One day—snap."

"HOW MUCH?" my stepbrother had wanted to know when I told him about the surgery. He still had no job, was on Ontario Works, and my mother paid for his meds. I didn't think I should tell him, so I just said it had cost a lot. I heard the cast clunk against the hard plastic handset of the phone as he altered his grip. When he punched the guy, he had fractured his wrist and it hadn't healed right, so they'd had to operate, break it again, put in pins to hold the narrow bones. It was his left hand, the one he used to draw.

No one—not him, nor my mother or sister—had ever asked us about euthanasia, but I could tell it was on their minds. "He's only three," I repeated again and again, whenever anyone actually asked or even hinted that they were wondering why we'd spent all that money, even though Barry Allen was probably closer to five, the vet had told us. What else could we do?

"ARE THERE NO HEROES anymore?" my mother had asked after the fight happened. Forgetting the time difference, she called me at eight on a Saturday morning, which was seven for us.

Beside me, Luke groaned, slapped a pillow over his exposed ear. I slipped out of bed, walked through the kitchen, drew the heavy green curtains in the living room to let in all the sunlight as she spoke. He'd been out at the skate park, she said. There were kids all around, kids he knew, who knew him, that he hung around with even though he was in his late twenties. They'd all watched, struck still and scared, as this man pushed himself against a woman on a nearby bench, his hand clutching the back of her neck. "It was subtle," my mother said, "easily overlooked." But kids are like that: they see. My stepbrother did, too, so he walked right up to them, right up to the woman's pale, scared face, and asked if there was a problem.

My mother told me the police arrived, and I imagined the man holding one hand against his bloody nose, pointing with the trembling fingers of the other. It turned out he was a lawyer and he charged my stepbrother with assault. By then, the woman had disappeared, ushered off by a female officer.

"Did she actually need help?" I asked.

"She had a black eye," my mother said. "You could see it from far off."

When I was there, in the courtroom, a lawyer in a silk blouse, brown skirt, read out a letter the woman had written, thanking my stepbrother. I watched him stare at the floor, his face drawn, indifferent. When she finished, he looked up into the room's sudden, momentary silence like he thought he'd heard something, was listening for a movement in the woods, then dropped his gaze back down to the polished tiles, the grid of dark lines. They gave him twenty hours of community service and a stupid anger management course.

"Like assaulted women shouldn't upset you," my mother snapped, her cheeks and forehead flushed red.

"Hush," his lawyer said.

I knew the judge had been lenient, but it didn't even matter because a week after that, my stepbrother checked himself into the hospital again. He'd been fired from his part-time job cleaning classrooms and hallways at an elementary school and was unable to draw because of his broken wrist. "Down inside the cobwebs," he told me. That was how he described it, how he'd explained it to me since I was eight and he was ten and he moved into my life when my mother married his father: like entering the sticky lair of those giant spiders in *The Hobbit*, the ones whose language only Bilbo could understand, and only when he wore the ring.

WE PICKED UP our mail from the post office—a final bill from the vet, for the prescription for tramadol, and a birthday card, two months late, from my sister. I hoped for a cheque as I broke open the paper edge of the envelope with my pinky, but the card just said *love and I hope everything's okay* in her leaning, hasty scrawl. We bought the wine, dropped my books—mostly mysteries and cookbooks—into the library bin, then turned around to drive back over the bridge, past the mall, the casino, and into the butcher's potholed parking lot. Smoke billowed past a line of tall, skinny spruce trees behind the building, and the air smelled like roasting meat. The butcher also operated a crematorium for animal remains, including people's family pets, because the veterinarian in town just sent them to the dump. That was the rumour, anyway, but really, what else could the vet do with those abandoned bodies?

"That pig sure smelled good," said the butcher as I set the marrow bones on the counter.

The plastic bag fogged from the warmth in the room. Luke poked through the other freezers, gathered up cheese smokies, a pound of pickerel cheeks, and set them down with the bones.

"You going tonight?" the butcher asked, as Luke walked away again and returned with blueberries, the wild ones, hand-picked farther north, where the Canadian Shield juts out of the earth.

I wanted to tell him to put them back, we'd just buy the cheaper no-name kind, but I didn't. "Maybe," I said.

"You got tickets?" He rang through a twenty-dollar sirloin Luke had added to the pile, and I watched his big fingers, ticked with white scars, tapping the black buttons on the cash register. The total was nearly our full weekly budget for groceries, before we'd even bought tea, onions, dog kibble, or other staples, but I just handed over my credit card. "'Cause it's sold-out," he said.

"Well, that's that, then," I told him. I didn't really care. I'd already let it go and was doing math in my head, tallying the accumulation of Air Miles I'd earn with this latest expense, how many more I would need for another flight back home.

IF IT WEREN'T for us and a couple others, Barry Allen would be dead. There was the nurse who pulled him out of Cross Lake on the day of a cull, when they shoot the stray dogs who have packed up. He was a year old, and on his shoulder was a large patch of shiny silver scar tissue from a burn caused by hot oil, tossed to scare him away. Still, he loved people.

The nurse had bundled Barry Allen and his sister, Buffy, who ended up with a family in Flin Flon, into a minivan and drove out as a gun popped twice behind them. She'd almost gone off the red earth road, she was so hysterical. This woman who worked the emergency room, who could splint shattered bones, hold blood inside a body.

The animal rescue in town called us because we were on a list to foster, and Barry Allen came straight to our place. The first night all he wanted was to go outside, into our tiny fenced yard shared with the old lady upstairs. He bucked around endlessly on the leash, dug at his blue collar with his claws. It took a while, but he calmed after a few days and started to show his goofy, friendly side, so we fell for him. Now, deaf in one ear and with arthritis in both knees and an elbow, he's still our firstborn, our kid.

WHEN WE PULLED into the driveway, Barry Allen started to bark. We could hear him through the walls of the house. Luke shut off the truck. A light snow, only the second of the season, fell on the windshield, the tiny, fine flakes melting in the watery spread of low sun.

"Do you want to go?" he asked.

"Where?"

He could have meant anywhere: back to town to get the barbecued chicken, home to Ontario, south to Las Vegas on a cheap flight from North Dakota.

His hand stayed on the keys, playing with the blue magpie feather I'd found on the lawn in the summer and bound with a leather cord. "The thing," he said. "The supper."

I looked out at the tamarack beside the driveway, the needles so yellow they resembled pink gold. Winter would strip them, transform the branches into a lonely sketch against the white.

I turned back and saw how Luke was waiting for me, his face like I'd seen it at the vet's, eager and scared as they walked Barry Allen out to us with his left leg shaved, ears back, eyes squinting until he spotted us, and his tail, despite everything, despite it all, started swinging hard, his leathery shoulder scar gleaming like a badge under the fluorescent lights. I hadn't mentioned that part to my stepbrother: how much we loved him, how much he loved us. How looking after him in that narrow pen had shrunk my world to a singular purpose, given me an obvious few square feet in which to root.

"Okay," I said, because I knew he was up to something, and his face relaxed.

He reached across my lap, which was piled with paper bags from the butcher, to the glove box and pulled out two tickets. "To Hawaii," he said, and I put my hand over my mouth.

"HE'S BAD AGAIN," my mother had told me a week earlier, when I talked to her over Skype. Her face melted occasionally into a watery smear like an impressionist painting, but I still saw the tremble in her chin. Her ex-husband—my stepfather, I suppose you'd call him—had moved to London, England, two years before to be with a woman he'd met on the internet. He spoke to my stepbrother only at Christmas, sometimes on his birthday.

"He's not even my kid, but I can't just abandon him," I'd heard my mother say again and again.

Neither could I. We were close; we were accidental siblings but also friends.

"He's hardly leaving the house," she said. "All he does is play online poker and drink that awful cheap whisky."

"Is he winning?"

It was the wrong thing to say. Instead of answering, she pushed her fingertips into the roots of her fine hair, and I mimicked the movement, felt the bumps in my skull beneath the tight skin. When I stopped, she was staring at me, the screen snapped suddenly clear so I could see details you normally only get in person: the scrape of mascara through her long lashes, delicate clumps like blackflies caught in a web, and her faded coral lipstick.

"It'll be okay," I said, even though I didn't know if that was true.

She lifted a red-and-white mug covered with a snowflake pattern to her mouth, then asked about Luke, his job, and whether we'd be flying home for Christmas. In my stomach was the same cold nausea I felt late at night when I thought of our debt and Barry Allen's other knee, that invisible braided tendon slowly unravelling.

"No," I said.

"He's got nobody but us," my mother told me, as if I didn't know. "If I find the money, will you come?"

I WAS ON MY OWN and far from home when Barry Allen injured his leg. It was the first week of school, Luke back at work, an hour before my shift at the gym started. I'd taken him out by the lake where muskrats troll the weedy shallows and ducks explode out of tree boxes in the summer. He was running, a full sprint along the water's mucky edge, when he yelped. It seemed like nothing: the leg quickly raised, maybe a pulled muscle, and I tried to get him to step on it, to walk off the injury, but the limb dangled at his side as he looked at me, the skin of his face tight with stress. He couldn't put any weight on it. I had to carry him home.

I swear he knew what was happening because he went limp in my arms, all fifty pounds of him. His chin bobbed against my shoulder blade, his hot breath on my neck, as we trudged the path to the car. Every few minutes, I had to set him down for a break, and he'd stand there, his useless leg quivering in the air, pink tongue lolling out as he watched me, waiting. It took me an hour, a walk that's normally half of that, and then I had to stay with him. I couldn't go to work.

I WORE A SUNDRESS, bright yellow, covered with a garden of multicoloured flowers. It had cost over two hundred dollars, was purchased for my sister's quiet August wedding, and I'd moved it all the way up north in a garment bag because I had worn it only that once. I was glad to have another chance to put it on, even though it felt a bit snug. Probably from all the wine, the drinking we did up here that was way more than back home.

In the hotel dining room, a waitress I recognized from her weekend job at the library hung green-and-blue plastic leis around our necks. Her grass skirt bristled as she moved, and her T-shirt, a tourist one, faded blue with orange print that said *Acapulco*, stretched across her breasts. It looked like a relic from the eighties, like something my mother might have worn to work in the garden. Luke's hand hovered on the small of my back as she led us to a table in the corner beside an inflated palm tree and then cleared the surface of another couple's greasy plates and a drained carafe of red wine.

The pig lay in the middle of the buffet table, a red apple in its mouth. Its posture reminded me of a dog's play stance, arms out flat on the ground, but I suppressed any squeamishness and pulled off a few ounces of pink meat. The butcher was right: it smelled delicious, and tasted succulent and salty next to the sweet of grilled pineapple.

After our main course, Luke ordered two glasses of champagne. The eagerness in his face, the intensity of his gaze, gave it away when I felt the hard thing hit my teeth. It was the size of a small creature's vertebra. I took it briefly into my mouth, onto my tongue, before sending it back into the glass, peering down through the bubbles at the gleaming gold band, the small diamond's icy glimmer. Here? was the first thing I thought, glancing outside to get my bearings. The window was fogged with condensation, hiding a world still grey and cold despite the colours, the cardboard and plastic foliage, the fake sunshine all around.

ON THE DRIVE HOME, I sat in the centre of the seat, my legs on either side of the stick shift, pressed against Luke in the small space of the cab. My fingers were sticky from fishing the engagement ring out of my drink, and between our intertwined hands was this sudden hard circle of gold. I felt nervous, but I also couldn't stop smiling, caught up in the warm rush of that artificial vacation, the celebration as the waitresses had come by to clear our plates, brought slices of chocolate cake with the icing glowing under small pink candles. Somebody asked if we'd set a date, but I didn't want to think that far ahead, to the threshold after which would come the rest of my life: other dogs, even babies, a house of our own in this town where we'd lived for only one year, a town that felt so far from where I thought I actually belonged.

In the driveway, Luke kissed me, his mouth a hot centre of the gravity that had drawn me north with him after he got hired for the only teaching job he could find. "You'll be free," my sister said when I told her about his plans and my uncertainty. In order to avoid an argument, I agreed with her because in truth I didn't have that particular desire, to get away, the urge that had sent her all the way out west, halfway to Japan. Luke, an only child, saw the move as an adventure, so I'd given in, let him convince me, and tried not to talk about regret.

I SAT IN THE CAGE with the dog while Luke called his parents to tell them our news. Barry Allen's fur was starting to thicken with the coming of the cold, and I took off his cone, buried my fingers in the nape of his neck. Before the surgery, we'd been offered a form to sign, giving the doctors permission to cut open Barry Allen's chest and massage his heart if they started to lose him, and although I had wondered at the astronomical cost, Luke hadn't even hesitated. The vet had looked on, calm and approving, his hand resting casually on the model of a functioning canine knee, as Luke pressed the stylus to the tablet and made his name appear, dark and authoritative.

"It's amazing what they can do now," my stepbrother had said when I explained the surgery to him over the phone, went deeper into detail in response to all his questions. I told him how they cut the tibia to alter the geometry so the bend no longer needed a tendon.

"Luckily his meniscus wasn't torn," I said, tapping my own kneecap. "It's the thing that cushions impact. That'll help him as he ages."

My brother had gone quiet, I remember. In the background I could hear the wailing of a distant siren, the chatter of a television playing *Jeopardy*. "What is Iwo Jima," he muttered, and then, when he finally spoke to me again his tone was gentle, almost admiring. "Lucky dog," he said, and I felt a lump in my throat that was hard and sturdy, as if I'd always had it, just sometimes didn't notice, like a bone spur that will never go away.

"Mom wants to talk to you," Luke said. The sound of his words lifted my head and Barry Allen's at the same time, so we moved together, me with my chin nestled into his coat. Luke's mother's excited voice continued on as Luke held out the handset, watching me, and I stood to step out of the cage. His face looked rosy and warm, green eyes lit from a grin he couldn't stop, helpless in his own happiness, like Barry Allen when we came home from work, when he pushed his snout into our hands, looking to be soothed, and we gave him all the affection we could, the three of us on his bed in the corner of the kitchen. Sometimes we ate dinner in there, offering him tidbits from our plates.

I took the phone from Luke's hand, and his mother blasted her congratulations, then started asking me all the questions I couldn't answer.

"Surely the wedding won't be out there," she said, and I shook my head, wondering suddenly what we would do with the dog, how we'd make it all work.

Then a beep sounded, announcing another call. "Hold on," I told Luke's mom, and even as I clicked over, I don't know how, but I knew. My stomach dropped. What went through my mind before I said hello was, *How will I ever be happy again?*

"You gotta get here," my mother said, her voice made of gravel, a harsh scrape against my soft ear, before she broke down. Her sudden, high-pitched sob made me think of that quick yelp Barry Allen had given, out in the lonely wilderness, announcing his useless, broken limb. A keening. The ground so suddenly gone.

Culture Shock

ight leans on the grass.

In the distance, past the weedy trough of a ditch, at the end of a winding dirt path, Ruth sees slivers of white.

The bus has already gone. She stands on the side of the road in more quiet than she's experienced since arriving in Argentina. Listening to the deep tone of the rural silence broken only by bird calls and a distant motor, an airplane flying far overhead, she is glad she came. Her body pulls air deep inside her lungs and pushes it out and she feels safe. Safe, despite being alone, in another hemisphere, in the opposite season, in a country where she can't speak the language. And, now, in the middle of rural nowhere.

Only this morning, she'd read about the old Jesuit chapel in her travel guide and decided to come. To catch the bus and ask to be let out at the historic structure where an attendant sat in the shade, collected pesos, handed out pamphlets available in

English for a two-peso charge, according to her guidebook. It was an adventure, which was good, since she was already bored. Tired of wandering around Tucumán, where she'd arrived from Buenos Aires two days earlier, walking in circles while realizing it wasn't much of a place, just a quiet agricultural community where everyone stared at her, where she was foreign. The cathedral stood in the centre of town, and yesterday she'd aimed her camera at it, tipping the box this way and that, attempting to fit the spires inside the frame. When it didn't work, she broke the building into pieces. After that, she went back to her hotel, unsettled by the smell of urine and dust in the streets, the way the air was fogged with yellow exhaust, how the men, crowded into pickup trucks, stared at her. She was far, far away from Buenos Aires, with its other North American travellers, its glitz and sophisticated glamour, its wealth.

The others were going south. Everyone went south, to Patagonia. But Ruth wanted north, the mystery, the unknown. And so, three days ago, ready for the long bus ride, she'd hauled her backpack onto her shoulders and said goodbye to the other travellers in the hostel, sprawled on chairs in front of the TV in the common room, a plastic ashtray overflowing beside five empty beer bottles. The one girl, Sandy, an American from Ann Arbor, who Ruth had gone to the antiques market with, smiled and told her to have a good time.

"You, too," Ruth said. They exchanged email addresses, but Ruth knew that neither of them would write. That was the way of travelling. You existed and then you didn't, and in this way you learned that the world was not small.

So now it is a relief to be alone, no one staring or sizing her up, no act of nonchalance needed as eyes rake over her in the middle of the night at a bus station or on the street in the city. Such hardness makes her feel lonely. Once, in Buenos Aires, on the subway platform, she'd softened to ask a woman for directions, and within two minutes six people had gathered around to help her find her way. It had felt impossible to stay impervious, invulnerable, so she allowed herself to relax and be grateful as they argued among themselves over the best route. When the crowd dispersed, she walked back through the gate to get on the correct train, feeling light inside, no longer carrying lead. Her armour had been shed, but as the day wore on, she sensed that it had exposed her to some potential danger, so she avoided the eyes of strangers again, hunched her shoulders as if walking to work in Toronto, and wished it could be different.

But that was part of what she wanted. To be scared; to be cracked open. To disturb the cold layer that had settled itself over her nine-to-five life, one day stitched to the next until the sudden emptiness of the weekend arrived and Ruth found herself drinking with her friend Lily, hungover on Sunday or Saturday or both.

"Feeling all right?" Lily would ask in the afternoon when she called, the same stupid joke they'd lobbed back and forth since high school.

Lately, though, Ruth found she didn't have the words to describe the abyss that had started opening inside her. Instead, she faked it, played along. "What did I do last night?" she groaned, reading from an invisible script.

"Should I tell you?" Sharp inhale of a cigarette. Stabbing pain in Ruth's head. She ran cold water from the tap while Lily went on, all the while a big black hole stretching wide beneath Ruth's heart that nothing could fill. She tried. She poured more beer into it, swarmed its walls with smoke from Lily's loosely rolled joints and her cigarettes, but it stayed hollow and cold until it seemed there wasn't anything—not even the predictable persistence of pain—that could alter the course she was on. On Monday mornings, on her way to work, she stood, tender with the familiar ache, and blinked into the soundless chasm of the subway car.

At night, lying in bed, she thought about emptiness. Her emptiness. It frightened her, and the fear tried to propel her to the doctor, to force her into opening her mouth and pleading for Prozac or Zoloft or something, some helpful drug. But Ruth didn't listen. Instead, she held to the fear, felt its edge, sharper and more real than the numbness that was slowly, like an approaching glacier, trying to cover any evidence of life until finally an answer emerged. *Get away*, a voice inside her said.

SHE HAD CHOSEN Tucumán because the photographs on the hostel wall showed desert, cacti, sculptured red rock. But she hadn't gone far enough north. Where she ended up was green and flat, and there was nothing to do but walk around the square, sip coffee in the cantinas, and sit on the balcony of her hotel room reading and looking out over the palm trees and bougainvillea in the courtyard, trying to figure out what to do next.

THE WHITE CHAPEL gleams through green foliage. Ruth walks the dirt trail toward it. Birds rise chaotically out of tree branches and a car speeds by on the road behind her, going so fast she's sure its passengers can't see her. A branch cracks underfoot, startling her, and she stops walking. She hears nothing. No voices up ahead, just the strange calls of species she can't name. The place is empty, no attendant manning a table, opening his hand for her few pesos. No one. The mid-January sun is hot, but she shivers, staring at the plaster walls of the chapel on the far side of the clearing.

It's a church, Ruth, she says to herself, stepping forward.

Everyone's welcome at a church.

ONCE SHE'D DECIDED to leave, Ruth bought her ticket quickly. She sat down with a travel agent, her heart beating hard as she flipped the pages of a small calendar on the agent's desk and decided on dates. She wanted to go for a month. She realized she would have to quit her job, and that decision brought relief, a pure cool flood of it. What would she do when she got back? What about her apartment? She decided to travel for two months, then three.

"Is it cheap there?" she asked the travel agent. The gold pin on the woman's red blouse said *Maria* in black letters, but Ruth couldn't bring herself to say her name, to imagine an intimacy that wasn't really there.

"Cheap? Inexpensive? No, not really," the travel agent said. "You'll be paying mostly in American dollars." She looked up from her keyboard and smiled. "Well, in Buenos Aires, anyway."

Ruth did some math in her head and decided to drain the last of her savings account, then to sell all her stuff.

THIS MORNING, at the station, Ruth had twice repeated the name of the bus the guidebook told her to catch before the attendant nodded and slid a ticket under the clear panel.

She bought two peaches, an empanada, and a bottle of water, then waited in the shade, trying to ignore the clutch of men standing in the corner wearing baseball caps and long-sleeved shirts, staring at her. They laughed, and a knot tightened in her stomach. On the way there she'd walked by several eyes, kept her own anchored on the end of the street, on the plumes of exhaust rising from the buses' big metal bodies. Now and then she lifted her camera to snap an image of the old colonial buildings, their shingles crumbling, their splintering bodies turned into stores for cheap electronics or fruit stands where women wore flowered aprons and held out melons, bunches of bananas as she walked by.

Ruth boarded the bus when it came, squeezing one foot in front of the next, moving around elbows and knees, children hanging into the narrow aisle, a lone silent person in the midst of conversations and laughter and life. Salsa music blared from the speakers. She headed toward an empty seat near the back, across the aisle from a nun, her head bent in what Ruth at first thought was prayer but was actually a palm full of candy offered to a child hidden by the tall seat. She sat down and looked out the window, saw that the group of men had broken up and two of them were walking toward the nearby cantina, its doors swung open, the inside dark.

The driver made an announcement that Ruth didn't understand before they pulled out onto the road. The vehicle swayed around a corner and started to shake as the driver picked up speed. Her finger holding her place in the pages of the guidebook, Ruth watched a rosary swinging from the rear-view mirror. Nervously, she wondered if the driver had notified the passengers of a short stop, a change in the route, and suddenly thought of all the people in Toronto who couldn't speak English, what their lives might be like. Confusion; arriving someplace you didn't mean to go to. Lost.

WHEN RUTH TOLD LILY about her trip, Lily's eyes narrowed.

"Are you nuts?" she asked. She spun a finger beside her right ear. "You know? Loco?"

Ruth took a drag of her cigarette and shrugged. That morning, on her way to work in the drab office where she answered the phone and opened the mail, she had felt buoyed by the knowledge of her trip, by the decision to quit her job and leave her apartment, her life. But later, on the subway, she'd felt herself deflate as she watched the sad faces staring out the grimy windows. She'd heard it, the low hiss of a slow leak, and that night she heard it again, in the bar with Lily, watching her friend's face contort into a scowl, her mouth opening to toss large obstacles in Ruth's way.

After that, whenever Ruth mentioned anything about her trip, Lily carefully changed the subject, turned Ruth's attention elsewhere by offering her a smoke or ordering another pitcher of beer. But Ruth whispered the name to herself while Lily was in the washroom. "Ar–gen–ti–na," she breathed, spinning the orange ember of her cigarette in circles against the ashtray's glass edge. Ruth wondered what she would find there: the revelation of a path, some meaning, some way to shed the stifling skin she'd started to wear.

RUTH WATCHED the green fields slide by, the flat landscape broken by cement-block houses and gravel roads. This was the right thing, she thought, whether the driver remembered to let her off or not. Wherever she ended up, she knew how to get back. The guidebook explained it: get off the bus, cross the road, and wave down another bus heading back into Tucumán. It was all right. She took a deep breath and felt her nerves begin to settle as the bus slowed onto the gravel shoulder and shuddered to a stop. The door opened. An old woman carrying a basket and wearing a red blouse shot through with metallic thread climbed on board.

Ruth watched her move slowly up the aisle, one hand clutching the backs of the seats to keep her balance as the driver pulled back onto the road. The woman sat down next to Ruth and set the basket, full of apples, small and yellow, one marked by a brown hole, on her lap. Ruth turned back to the window and watched the view pass by.

"A dónde va?" someone said.

"A dónde va?" she heard again. The woman was speaking to her. Ruth smiled, embarrassed, and the woman smiled, too, deepening the crow's feet around her eyes, which were close enough that Ruth could see her own tiny reflection hovering upside down in the woman's black pupils.

"Canada. Toronto," Ruth said.

The woman blinked. Beside her the nun was talking to the little girl.

"Ah," she said. "Bueno. Pero a dónde va?"

"Oh," Ruth said, understanding. The question meant where was she going, not where was she from. She lifted the guidebook and pointed to the passage about the chapel. The woman touched the book to hold it still and squinted at the lines of text until Ruth took it back, looked more carefully, and said the name out loud: "Ruines de San Jose de Lules."

A deep crease stitched itself across the woman's forehead. She reached out and tapped a finger, hard, on the open pages of the book. "Hay perros!" she blurted, brown eyes intent on Ruth, almost angry. One of the apples fell to the floor with a dull thunk and rolled away. The woman ignored it, tapping again on the image of the chapel in Ruth's book, repeating the words.

"No entiendo," Ruth said. "Perdone, no entiendo." She lifted her hands to show her helplessness, wishing she'd remembered her Spanish–English dictionary. The woman sighed heavily and shook her head. People were turning to stare and speak to the woman, who answered back, voice raised, her words sharp in the heavy, hot air of the bus. Ruth turned toward the window, lifted her mouth to the narrow crack to try to find some fresh air.

When the bus pulled over at an inconspicuous spot along the straight stretch of asphalt, she saw the driver's eyes watching her in the rear-view mirror, waiting. Ruth stood and squeezed past the knees of the old woman, who crossed herself and lifted a small yellow apple up for Ruth to take.

"No, gracias," Ruth said. She was allergic; she'd get hives. It was too much to explain. The woman shook her head, irritated, Ruth could tell, and muttered something as she returned the apple to her basket. Ruth walked to the front of the bus, the passengers quietly watching. The driver pointed to an opening in the woods, the shadowy mouth of a trail, and before she descended, she glanced toward the back, toward the old woman. Eyes closed, lips moving in a secret prayer, hand lifting to cross herself, as Ruth stepped down into the dust.

LILY, RUTH THOUGHT, was jealous. She hadn't been anywhere, only on a spring-break trip to Florida years ago with Ruth. Ruth had been west to B.C. and Seattle, and a day's drive east to Quebec City, as well as an all-inclusive trip to the Dominican Republic with her mother and stepfather when she turned nineteen. In the days before she left for Argentina, she started realizing she couldn't share anything with her so-called best friend. As they sat at their usual table in the back corner of the dimly lit bar, she kept her plans to herself, held the trip like a candy she rolled around in her mouth, tasting all the names of the towns and cities she wanted to see. Jujuy, Córdoba, Salta. She repeated rudimentary Spanish words and phrases—yo soy Ruth, cómo estás?—until she started to feel different, like she could be somebody else. Like she used to feel when she and Lily started drinking and it was fun. How her body loosened. How she could let herself go; how she was slowly, ecstatically opened to the point of feeling truly free. But that was before. Before she began waking up into stifling darkness, lungs aching, her heart a sodden weight in her chest.

THE STUCCOED CHURCH stands in a clearing of packed brown dirt. Ruth aims her camera at a pile of red clay shingles fallen to the ground, and the door, a black gap in the whitewashed wall.

Inside, she waits for her eyes to adjust. Slowly, shapes come clear. Scaffolding stands against the back wall, behind the altar, and Ruth looks up to the high frescoed ceiling and sees the faint glint of a gilded sun.

Is this why the woman had prayed? Because the chapel is a holy place—not for foreigners, not for Ruth? She steps farther into the cool dark, head tipped back, examining the colours and painted detail, imagining the story she will try to tell Lily when she goes home, of finding this place, of travelling into the middle of nowhere, of being brave. But she knows Lily won't listen, won't care. Two days before Ruth was to leave, Lily had left her passed out on a park bench where she woke to the cold stab of dawn, a cop shaking her ankle. She shivers with shame at the memory. She isn't even Catholic, but she lifts her arm to cross herself, fingertips touching forehead and chest, nudging against each shoulder.

As her hand falls to her side, she hears a noise. Her eyes dig into the space where the long, narrow church is darkest, and she sees them: two tiny pinpricks of light. Then the glare of teeth. And now she hears a growl.

Fear is in her stomach. She listens, and it tells her what to do. Drop her eyes, bend her knees. Crouched, she shuffles backward, like an animal retreating from another's territory.

The dog comes closer, stalking the length of the building toward her. The sound in its throat, that low, terrifying growl, grows into crazed barking that rings in the high space of the church. She doesn't look. Her gaze scrapes the earthen floor as she grovels, pushing down as hard as she can on the heavy drowning weight of her fear, clutching for the memory of that gold sphere high above her head and the old woman crossing herself on the bus. She doesn't expect it, but it fills her, the memory. It inflates her. It lifts her above the terrible drowning darkness of her fear and tells her what to do—*turn around, move steadily*—even as the dog gets closer, its breath hot on her leg.

At the back of the church, another dog growls, then a third. Suddenly, there is only this: the narrow bridge between dark and light.

Places Like These

For weeks, I have been seeing Robert. Turning the corner of the grocery store as I walk in for frozen dinners and yogurt, disappearing into subway cars. Always he is wearing that light brown jacket he had in the eighties and a pair of worn, baggy blue jeans. He looks like he did the summer of '88, when we took the train to Moosonee, when we began travelling, started spending money on ourselves, when we gave up, as my mother called it right up until she died.

"He has a message for you," Joanie told me, and said I should go. Three times in one week I heard about the place: the article in the doctor's office, when I went for my mammogram and flipped open *Budget Travel* to those glossy pictures of the community's iron gate, the summer-camp-like amphitheatre, and a medium peering down at her spread of tarot cards; then there was a book face up in a sidewalk remainders bin, bearing a black-and-white image of Victorian psychics; and finally, the reassuring baritone of Michael Enright's voice on the radio —*Next up, a town where the dead can talk*—reverberating through my quiet apartment as I walked, towel-clad, to take a shower. I froze, leaned a naked shoulder against the plaster wall, felt a shiver under my skin. "You have to go," Joanie said. "He is close. Even I feel that."

IN THE HOTEL LOBBY, a framed sign says *Absolutely No Séances!* It's crooked, hung on a wood-panelled pillar. A dusty Persian carpet is spread on the hardwood floor beneath a set of wicker furniture. The pink-and-red cushions clash with the rug. The place is old, smelling of mildew overlaid with the cloying fragrance of artificial vanilla from the plug-in air freshener. Out on the front veranda, half a dozen rocking chairs thump against the hollow floor. I hear people chattering, mostly women with their daughters and girlfriends, eager to reach their loved ones, find the person who can penetrate the distance, pull back the dead as if hauling fish from the depths. I'm the only one who seems to be alone, apart from a skinny white-haired man in polyester tan pants, thick-soled white shoes, and a plaid flannel shirt, even now, even in the high humid summer. He's sitting on the wicker love seat, looking down. Against his leg he presses a glossy brochure, and even from all the way over here, in line for my turn at the desk, waiting to receive an iron skeleton key with a large purple plastic tag marked 42 in worn gold numbers, I see the tiny image of a woman, hair short and black in a polished cap like a beetle's carapace. I wonder if she's the one I'm meant to go to, if spotting her miniature, smiling face like this, like a slight, secret thought that pulls you up into consciousness in

the empty wasteland of the night, is a sign. But when I turn back
from scrawling my signature in the register, he is gone.

ROBERT HAD HIS HEART attack after our trip to B.C. We'd hiked
too much, eaten too much rich food. Oysters dredged through
bowls of foamy, golden garlic butter; hard walks over the forest's
uneven floor. Everything was my idea, even the tent trailer—a
two-person contraption with shrunken canvas that dragged
behind us as we floored the mushy gas pedal up through the
Rockies. Robert clenched the steering wheel, eyes flickering to
the rear-view, embarrassed at the lineup building behind us.
"Just put on your hazards," I said, exasperated, and his finger
trembled as he fumbled for the button on the dash, pressing it
firmly like a final decision. By then, we'd been married for eighteen years, and there were cracks, subtle ones like the settling of
foundation cement, not deep enough to do damage. "Like a house,"
I told my sister, Joanie, who at fifty-one had never married,
though she had birthed a child at sixteen, back home in Hearst,
and given him up for adoption. Last autumn, after I was wid-
owed, she was in the flush of new motherhood because he had
found her, sent a card with a wide, choppy ocean on the front, a
miniature dinghy carrying a little blond-haired girl and an
orangutan, rowing. The card was creased, as if purchased years
ago, never sent. "Strange choice," I said. "He's a veterinarian,"
she told me. Her eyes had not stopped shining.

THE WALLS IN MY ROOM are covered in climbing green vines
and pink rose blooms that look like they've faded from red.

There's a double bed with shrieking springs. The coverlet is cream-coloured, with a nubby texture and a silky fringe. There is a sink in the corner, with old-fashioned taps, and shared showers and toilets across the hall. Through the single small window I can see a row of yellow, blue, and white Victorian houses, trimmed in gingerbread. Shingles hang over their stained-glass-panelled doors: *Animal Medium, Tarot Card Readings, Spirit Message Work.* I let the sheer white curtain fall and dim the sun. It is a beautiful August afternoon; I really should be outside. Through the metal screen, I hear happy, distant voices, and a woman at the microphone in the amphitheatre. "I'm getting an M," she says. "I see a pile of books by a bed."

ROBERT AND I HAVE no children. We tried for years. When nothing happened but my regular period, showing up each month like a surly, passive teenager, I went to an acupuncturist and drank cup after cup of bitter, dirt-tasting tea, a different one each week. In his office, I shrank back on the cold cot as he threaded stainless-steel needles through my skin. Whenever he hit a point of built-up tension, I felt the release like pure electricity, like a fingertip glancing an open circuit. It was uncomfortable. All that time, those long years, trying that and even more, were uncomfortable. Robert told me it didn't matter, but I could never believe him, was not convinced that inside himself he didn't harbour regret, like sediment gathered in his blood. One day, it drifted into his heart, and that's what killed him.

My sister shook her head when I first made this confession. She is a nurse, pragmatic, practical, always searching out the obvious. "He loved you," she told me then, wanting to reach for my hand but resisting. Her fingers closed gently into a fist on the table's edge. "He would have done it all over in a heartbeat." The exact words he often used. Maybe she'd heard him say it.

WE DIDN'T BOTHER stopping in Vancouver. It would have been a nightmare driving through with the trailer—all those busy streets and last-second turns. At Horseshoe Bay, we caught the ferry to Nanaimo, took the space of two cars. Robert didn't want to leave the driver's seat. In hindsight, I think he was already getting ill, his face pasty and grey, a sheen of oily sweat on his brow. How he kept licking his lips. *I should have known* is what I want to say, what I want to somehow tell him, and also, *I'm sorry, for the life I gave you, the loneliness you never expected.* In the back of the car, his fishing gear was piled up, a special salt-water rod that wouldn't rust, that he'd just bought. Gently, with the promise of soup and a cup of coffee, treacly sweet the way he liked it, a treat of eighteen percent cream, I enticed him to the upper decks. Outside, the wind was so strong, it lashed the sharp points of my hair into my eyes. We sought the shelter of the ship's lee side and, alone on the deck but for the cigarette smokers and a young man with long hair that looked dry as hay, a pipe hidden in his cupped hand, we saw the killer whales. Two of them, breaching side by side, and after they dove down, a momentary pool of stillness appeared in the ocean's dark churn. I gripped Robert's cold hand and warmed it between my own as we stood against the railing, the smell of marijuana like incense in the air.

I WAKE, ALONE, in the late afternoon. I am still not used to the hollow that my body pushes against, the empty air where once there was form. Robert's girth, broad-shouldered, a hefty gut on him from the time he turned forty-five. Nowadays everyone says that's a sign, but we were never ones to baby our mortality. From the time we were young together, we enjoyed food, didn't restrict its pleasures: ate butter, fried foods—in balance, I suppose, with organic greens and grapeseed oil in place of olive in the pan in later years. We didn't smoke, drank too much only during those two years in Hudson Bay, Saskatchewan, when Robert was getting his start in the newsroom and there was nothing else to do. We were in our thirties then. Who doesn't do that?

"Genetics," Joanie often says. "You can't fight 'em."

She says that for me but also for herself, as a way to shift the conversation. I've heard it all before, but I smile whenever she tells me again: the remarkable way her son, Allan now when she had named him Stuart, swings his hand to the right, fingers flipped out, in the exact same dismissive gesture she uses, how his forehead creases like hers when he's listening hard.

Robert's father died at fifty-eight. A massive heart attack in the underground quarry in Goderich, where he worked as foreman. They found him face down on the edge of a snowdrift of salt. The air glimmering and sharp, I imagine, because I've been there, because Robert and I did a tour of that place on another, different trip.

THE TRAIL TO Inspiration Stump leads through the pet cemetery, which isn't kept up. Purple-blooming periwinkle winds around a leaning wooden cross that says *Fluffy* in a scrawl of black paint. A clay angel sits, half melted from the rain, on the edge of the forest of tall hardwoods. Through the trunks, there is the constant shuffling of leaves, the flash of sunlight and shadow, the flicker of ribbons tied to low branches.

In the clearing, I sit on a bench for the final service of the day. Most of the people there must have eaten, because it's my stomach that growls into the silence as the medium climbs on top of the large trunk, his eyes closed, concentrating. He leans his ear toward the audience. Embarrassed, I press the palms of both hands against my roiling insides, trying to shush my hungry belly's complaints.

"You," says the medium. "You in the black shirt, green scarf."

I am curled into myself, around my hollow core.

"You," he says again, and someone nudges my shoulder.

"Honey, it's you!"

I look up.

"Kathy," he says.

I shake my head. "No."

Three women call out: "I'm Kathy! That's me!"

The medium looks flustered, a wash of pink in his cheeks. His eyes slide to the woman to my left, a gap the width of two bodies between us. Her face is tipped up, mouth slack. A friend clutches her hand, and their entwined fingers press against Kathy's bare, bony knee. "I see a dog," the medium says, and Kathy squints as she searches her mind.

"My cousin had a dog. He died last year."

"Ronnie, Rowan..." the medium mumbles.

"Robby," says Kathy.

I stare at her, then back at the medium.

"You loved this animal. You miss him. You walked with him." He pushes his fingers against his forehead, pinching the skin over his skull. "I see water."

Kathy looks confused.

Slowly I raise my arm, but the medium does not see me. Someone in the back has leapt up. "I had a dog named Ronnie," she shouts, and someone behind me gasps. "When I was a child," she says, and bursts out crying, cupping her mouth, nose, and chin in both hands. Weeping, she drops to the hard seat as the medium tells her it wasn't her fault, this is the message he's getting from the small grey terrier he can see now, and I stand up, push past Kathy, excusing myself, a quiver in my nerves, heart trembling, as I walk back through the woods.

YOU COME TO PLACES like this and expect to be called on. You come, expecting glimmering eyes to fall on you, flutter closed, and a voice to speak, clear enough to not be questioned: I see him, newly passed, and he wants me to tell you he loves you, he does not blame you, you were his best friend. The trip to B.C. was the best trip ever. Those walks on Chesterman Beach. The fires at the campground in Tofino. The afternoon out on the ocean, fishing for mackerel and salmon, a surprise for his birthday. All of it. He loved it.

He loved you.

At the cemetery I stop and sob like I'm barking, like part of me has something serious to say. There is no one there, so I sit on a tiny bench beside a gravestone bearing a framed picture of a black mastiff, deep jowls on his face, and let it out. The voices march on at the gathering, prodding great distances, but I came looking for one I'll never hear again, the reminiscing we would have done in later years, cancelling out the stress of the extra weight we were pulling, the real fear we felt when we hiked up the stony coast and the tide came in, unexpected. Turning it all into adventure. The revision that time can do.

I GO IN SEARCH of supper, but it's too late. All the little restaurants set up in former parlours, serving cranberry tea and apple pie to ladies on new-age book club retreats, have closed. There's only one answer and that's to drive toward town.

At the corner of the main highway and the road leading to Lily Dale, I find a tavern called Brixies Bar & Grill. In the parking lot, six Harley-Davidsons are lined up in a neat row, and I wonder if their riders had to work at that or if they'd gotten it right on the first try. If Robert was here, the sight of the bikes would make him nervous and his hesitation would bolster my nerve. For five minutes, I sit in the car, checking my phone to see if my sister has texted, but the screen is blank, apart from a picture of Robert, his features scarred by tiny icons. I slide the icons to the side so I can see his right eye, the glint in it, the laugh lines, one half of his smile. A fragment, still with me, a shard.

Inside the tavern, I see the old man from the hotel lobby. He sits at a table for two, one shoulder leaning against the wall, his shirt sleeves rolled up. His face is tipped into a book, and I watch his reflection in a huge mirror emblazoned with the Budweiser logo. We are on the dining room side, the only people there except for a couple and their small boy, who stabs a ball-point pen at the menu, screaming. The woman asks him once and then again, a shrillness growing in her voice, what he wants to eat. Her hands pat his chubby arms, trying to retrieve the pen as the man leans back, staring into his phone, thumbs jab-bing. "Dodged a bullet," Robert would have whispered to me over his beer, grinning.

I order a glass of red wine and a burger and fries without examining the menu and sit at an uncleared table. In the dim bar, the bikers are playing darts, slapping each other on their leather-clad shoulder blades, one in an olive drab T-shirt that says GREEN TEAM on the back. A baseball game is playing on the television. The man from the lobby holds a Caesar, rim crusted with fla-voured salt, a leafy rib of celery jutting out. He takes a drink, sets it down, and, with the fingers of his left hand, he pulls the psy-chic's brochure out of the pages of his book and lays it on the scarred surface of the table, tapping absent-mindedly on the image of her face as he reads. When he catches my gaze, he smiles tremulously, blinking twice before quickly looking away.

I lean sideways, extend an arm, trying to get his attention. "Excuse me," I say, and then when he doesn't look, I say, "Sir?"

He turns, the swivel of his head as slow as deep grief. His brown eyes are red-lined and watery, and he waits without speaking.

I decide to just say it: "Can I see that?"

He lifts the brochure. "This?"

I nod, and he looks at it, then me, then hands it over. The paper is slippery, and the sharp edge instantly gives me a paper cut. I flinch, press my stinging finger against an unused white napkin. Her name is Willa. She brings through identifiable spirit entities. I remember Robert's ashes, blown back by the wind. Our nephew, his youngest sister's son, lifting his small hands to catch the fine drift. "Have you used her?" I ask the man.

He scowls, then rocks in his chair, uncomfortable. "Well, no," he says. "She's my daughter."

I am startled. "Really?"

A curt nod.

I expect more: an enthusiastic recounting of how she always had the gift, but instead he returns to his book, then glances back. "I'm just visiting. From South Dakota. Where I have a ranch." Each sentence its own issued truth. Voice strained, like it hurts his throat to speak, he asks, "And you?"

Right then the waitress comes with my drink, a halo of light around her blond hair from the video lottery terminals, and past her I see movement, between the bar and the pool table, that tan jacket slipping out of sight. I almost stand up, almost shout out his name, but instead I take a gulp of wine as soon as the waitress sets the glass down.

"You all right?" the psychic's father says.

I sip the strong Merlot and turn to him as I'm breathing in through my nose, trying to smile. "I'm not sure," I say.

"I'm Wayne," he says, and he reaches across the gap between tables to shake my hand.

When we're parted, I ask, "Is she any good? I mean, I know you're her father, but…"

"I find..." He hesitates, then carefully turns down the corner of the page he is on in his book. A hardcover, blue, with a title I can't see, even when it's closed.

"Yes?"

"People find what they need."

"What do they need?"

He looks at me, eyebrows suddenly arched, his gaze sharpening onto mine. "I can't really answer that."

No, I think. Of course not. Disappointment washes through me, that wide, cold wave. I pick up my glass but find only a single swallow left. It stings the rawness of my throat.

WHEN THE TIDE gushed in, black and deep, on the day we hiked the coast, we didn't know what to do. Robert panicked, pacing back and forth on the small stretch of trail not blocked by ocean water. Around the corner, a short scramble over slippery rock, was the cove where we had eaten our lunch of pastrami sandwiches and carrot sticks and plain potato chips. It was the perfect spot: a firepit surrounded by driftwood benches, a dream catcher hanging overhead in an arbutus, a blackened and bent aluminum pot dredged in the fine sand, half full. And so that was where we spent the night: sleeping in each other's arms to keep warm against the cool, brine-smelling wind after we managed to build a fire, plucked blue mussels off the rocks, steamed them in sea water until their hinges released. It is my favourite memory of that trip, possibly of my whole life so far: watching the crescent moon pierce the sky over the ocean, my ear pressed to the buried, distant thump of Robert's beating heart.

Zombies

Julian just has to keep quiet.

He scribbles a blur of grey lead in the margin, counts to ten in his head.

The substitute teacher stops next to him, severing the line of white light that gleams through a crack in the closed, heavy curtains.

"Are you writing your answers down?" she asks, even though the tip of his pencil rests against a blank line, its yellow shaft latticed with tooth marks. Probably he should make an effort, but the questions are stupid: *What happens when there's more carbon dioxide in the atmosphere? What is happening to glaciers around the world?* He already knows the answers. They all do. This particular video, now outdated, he's seen six or seven times.

The first time, in Grade 7, Brittany, a cousin he barely knew, had come home from the University of Manitoba for their great-aunt's funeral. She brought the DVD because she had to watch it for school. They lay on their stomachs on his mom's bed, eating overheated strawberry Pop-Tarts, touching the sticky, leaking jam with their fingertips, waiting for it to cool as the movie played on the small, boxy TV set on the dresser. That day, after the burial, after Julian changed out of the polyester black pants bought at Giant Tiger and the too small dress shirt that smelled of old sweat, Brittany told him a lot. The film was outdated, she said. They were past the point of no return. The earth would overheat, towns and cities would flood, fires would burn. All they could do was watch.

He can't say that at school.

Once, he tried with Mrs. Fenner, the biology teacher, who isn't in today. He likes her, but all she did was smile in that artificial way, lips tight like they were drawn on her face. She didn't look at him when she said, "Well, we have to have faith, don't we?"

He knew then that she was just as blind as everybody else. It was lunch hour and he was feeding the fish, a couple other kids sitting at the back, making up a test they'd missed. He wanted to ask her what she meant by *faith*. He saw her lots around town in her SUV, a kayak tied to her roof racks, pulling through the McDonald's drive-through with her laughing, happy son.

But nothing else: she looked down at her work, scratched at the pages with her mechanical pencil, and he capped the green container of fish food, left, skipped his next two classes.

Last he heard, Brittany had moved to Toronto and was working for Greenpeace. Hustling people on the sidewalks, trying to raise money no one wanted to give. He wonders if she takes part in the climate strikes, has joined that movement, marched in the huge protest over inaction, thousands of people gathered in the city streets...to do what?

Stand with fists raised, in opposition to the system, the scaffolding that supports their own lives. If he could have, though, he would have gone, but he is stuck up here in the silent boreal, in this town like an island, peering through binoculars at the surprising, distant world. Seven hours to Winnipeg: the drive like rowing a boat, slowly, through a sea of black spruce. Only the occasional scavenging bear breaking the monotony, lazily hauling its head out of strewn roadside trash to calmly watch the passing cars.

IN THE CLASSROOM, the teacher has moved on. Julian pings his pencil off the metal leg of his chair and stops whenever she looks over. The rows behind him are occupied by kids face down on bent elbows, breathing on blank loose-leaf, sleeping, or else busy with their cellphones. Zombie gadgets, his grandfather had called them. The new girl—Coreen—is there, and he glances back at her, trying to catch her eye, but she ignores him, ignores everyone, hauling her body up to sitting to squint into the grey light when the teacher knocks sharply on the scarred surface of Coreen's desk.

When the sub gets back around to him, she holds out her hand for his pencil. He grips it in a curled fist, hangs his arm down by his leg.

"Would you like to go see Mr. Neville?" she asks.

Mr. Evil, the kids call him, but by Grade 11 the guy's no longer scary, just an old man hidden in his remote office.

"If you're not going to do the work," she says. "If you can't even bother caring—"

"Arctic sea ice just hit a record high," Julian blurts, staring at the screen hanging over the old-fashioned chalkboard. The colours are washed out, but he sees the brown river, the tobacco farm, Al Gore talking about his son's brush with death. "In melt, I mean," he clarifies.

The teacher stares at him, then shifts her eyes to look over his shoulder at the animal skeletons locked in a glass cage. For a second he thinks he might have reached her, that she might snap the light on, wake everyone up, get them talking. "I don't know about that," she says. "But your job today is to watch this film and answer—"

"It's twelve years old! This is *now*!" Julian nearly shouts, stabbing the top of his desk as if the environmental devastation is spread out before him. A mini-terrain of tar pits, poisoned ducks, polar bears, and walruses bobbing, dead and bloated, on a limitless Arctic Ocean, no ice in sight, an imaginary scene that reminds him of an acid trip he once went on with his buddy Rollo. A bad one, ending with Julian's gaze glued to the burning red dawn out on the Grace Lake dike, unable to move because he thought his feet had magnetized to the earth's iron core, six thousand kilometres below them, an unbelievably short distance, the thought of which, right then, had nearly blown his mind.

The teacher acts artificially calm. Arms crossed. A thread hangs from the cuff of her sleeve, and he sees now how it is worn, that edge, and stained. To Julian's left the redhead—Jenna, Jeanie, Jessie, whatever—is smirking.

"What are you looking at?" he says.

"Freak," she mouths.

"Fuck off," he tells her.

The sub sucks in a breath and marches to the front of the room. The film plays across her pale face as she hits the call button for the office. Julian stands, snatches the orange form from her hand, and leaves.

WHEN JULIAN WAS A KID, eleven or twelve, he met his grandfather most days after school in the spring and early fall. Upriver from the bridge, at the boat launch by the library. There were always guys there, cleaning jack and pickerel at the screened-in fish hut. Seagulls shifted like blown snow as his grandfather kicked through the flock in his big rubber boots, his stained pants rolled loosely to his knees. As he and the men talked, Julian watched the slender, steel blades slit the silver bellies, fingers digging out half-digested minnows and tangled line, discarding the guts into a battered aluminum garbage can. Stray dogs milled around, scrawny, legs caked with grey mud. His grandpa's brown hands dwarfed the tiny white sticks of cigarettes he smoked. Hand-rolled, made from loose, pungent tobacco.

AT THE OFFICE, Julian hands the form to Miss Schneider, who's sitting behind the tall desk. She takes it without comment, a phone pressed against her ear, and he listens to her talking about an anniversary social at the Legion, about making perogies. "At least six dozen," she says, and he feels suddenly starved, like he hasn't eaten for days. He skipped breakfast, belted down a quick bag of sour-cream-and-onion chips before gym, where the teacher shouted orders from her seat on the stage while she sucked on a straw sticking out of a Dairy Queen cup.

THE BELL RINGS, the classes shift, the hall fills with chattering, then grows quiet. Still, he sits, waiting at the end of a row of plastic chairs in the office. When the new girl, Coreen, comes in, he quickly straightens, squares his shoulders. She tosses the form, folded into the tiniest square possible, onto the surface of the desk. Miss Schneider looks right at her, blue eyes icy, and catches Julian's gaze for an instant before she reaches out and scoops up the form.

Coreen sits down and pulls a phone from the pocket of her stretched-out grey hoodie. Her black hair is streaked fuchsia; she's wearing scuffed army boots, torn red tights under a pleated plaid kilt, a shirt like a spiderweb stretched over a black tank top. There's a bruise, dark-purple-and-sulphur-coloured, on her cheek. Her phone pings before the screen goes blank and she groans, drops her hands into her lap, cradling the dead cell.

When she catches Julian looking at her, she returns his gaze, the thick bars of her eyeliner holding back all information. He wonders where she's from: Saskatoon or Pukatawagan, Brandon or Norway House. Her flat eyes invite his imagination, and he sees her in a sweaty mosh pit lit by roving orange and yellow lights, laughing, or walking barefoot with him through a poplar forest. Holding his hand. He turns away, feeling heat growing in his face, pretending he doesn't care at all—about her, about anything.

"Too short," she says, and lifts the hem of her skirt, flipping it up so he sees a ladder torn into her tights, and through its rungs, the skin of her thigh. His face grows hotter.

"You think so, too," she says. "Why's it up to me to wear a fucking hijab? Why's it not up to you assholes to control your fucking eyeballs?"

"Language," Miss Schneider scolds from behind the desk, her voice like a dull recording.

The girl leans over to whisper to him, and Julian feels himself sweating, a roiling starting up in his stomach, but right then Arnie Beauchamp walks in, grinning, and lifts his hand to fist-bump with Julian. He drops into a chair between Julian and Coreen, the orange paper rolled up in his fingers, crushed in the middle.

"What'd you do?" he asks, but Julian only shrugs. What's he supposed to say? *I talked out loud. I tried to communicate.* He's aware of the girl, sees her face go flat and hard as Arnie whispers something about calling it what it is, calling somebody a cunt. Julian nods, not really listening. The guy is nothing but an idiot who won't go anywhere, who'll end up working at the dump out past the mill or being a bouncer until he's stabbed on a Saturday night in the filthy, rowdy bar at the Cambrian Hotel.

Julian wants to go to university, to study biology or maybe politics, but he's not really sure how he's going to get there. By shutting up, he supposes. He's too much like his father, his mother has told him. Loves danger, the chaotic edges. It isn't really true. It's only a reason she makes up for the parts of him she doesn't understand.

HIS GRANDFATHER would gun the boat downriver, dead centre, curving around logs, mud flats. They'd go all the way to the estuary some days, if it was a weekend instead of a quick after-school trip, if they left early enough, if he could afford the extra tank of gas. He would give Julian a beer out of the cooler, but only one, sometimes two, and then he'd switch him to Orange Fanta. The fishing lines fell through the current's strong muscles, grew taut and shiny as they trolled. When the rods bent and jumped from a fish on the hook, his grandfather would get him to manoeuvre the loose steering wheel, to keep them on track while he stood on the grimy, carpeted floor, a big man in a small boat, sometimes unsteady even then because he was nearly eighty, and reeled in the flapping catch, tiring the fish before he netted it.

His grandfather didn't talk much. Mostly he was silent, unless he had jokes to tell, but Julian could read things in his face, in the places where his eyes lingered, on flattened patches of polished, pewter water or the drifting islands of muck and reeds the pelicans rode like rafts. Julian knew, from his grandfather's reactions, how things had changed, and, occasionally, rarely, from things he said, muttering after a long day in the sun and muscular wind when Julian again took the wheel and his grandfather leaned back on the wobbly, torn seat, speaking in a language Julian understood only in pieces. There aren't as many birds. The traplines are too often empty. Winter isn't really winter anymore or else it's too much winter and all the muskrats and springtime frogs freeze to death in their deep mud homes.

This, Julian thought, on top of everything. You take away a man's children, his language, his stories, his culture, his land, and now this: the seasons, the natural, ancient order. It enraged him.

"Julian."

He wasn't surprised when his grandfather died that September, drowned, having fallen out of his boat into the shocking cold of Clearwater Lake. Clumsy and looking for trout, he got tangled in his line, was hauled under a weight of icy water he didn't have the strength to fight.

"Julian?"

Coreen and Arnie are looking at him. The girl's gaze is calm, curious even, but her eyes fly away as soon as his swim over, as he rises out of his thoughts. He wipes his hands on the front of his jeans and stands.

"He doesn't have all day," Miss Schneider says, on her feet, pointing. "Go!"

The door at the end of the hall is open, and even from twenty feet away, Julian can see how the room contains only the autumn's murky light, pushing through the windows, the fluorescents shut off.

"Kick some ass," the girl says, and Julian turns to see Arnie look at her sharply, as if he hadn't even noticed she was there. She's braiding the bright pink lock in her hair, and for a second, she looks like a kid.

"I KNOW YOU'RE a smart young man," says Mr. Neville, resting a fingertip on the sheet, which is Day-Glo orange like something you'd wear in the bush to avoid being shot. A wound on the man's knuckle is red and seeping. "And I'm sorry for your loss."

Losses, Julian thinks, picking at his knee where his jeans are about to split. He digs out a loose thread, tugs harder. Mr. Neville is a skinny man, underweight, and his face is pale, smooth as milk except for the wrinkles gathered at the corners of his eyes like crumpled loose-leaf. A new moustache has formed on his upper lip, downy as chick feathers shed in the nest. Movember.

"But grief can't always be an excuse."

Julian stiffens. Mr. Neville doesn't notice. He weaves his fingers together, resting his hands on his desk. His gaze sits on Julian's face, steady and expectant, and Julian knows that all he has to do is give the right answer, the correct response, but his grandfather's voice echoes in his head. *Too many liars.*

"Here's the thing," says Mr. Neville. "You have to decide what you want, then put your mind to it, knuckle down." He drums the hollow desk, like Julian's own pencil beating out a forbidden rhythm back in class. On the wall, there's a poster of an eagle, the word INTEGRITY printed in large white letters beneath the soaring bird.

"Is that really true?" Julian asks.

"What?"

"That all I need to do is focus on what I want. Aren't there forces…?"

Mr. Neville's brow wrinkles suddenly, like a hard wind on water. "Forces?"

Julian says nothing. Mr. Neville leans back, and Julian senses how the man is unlatching his concern, preparing to give his pep talk.

"Well," he says. "That's always been the case, but it doesn't mean you just give up."

Julian works the hole in his pants wider, and finally Mr. Neville leans forward so he's almost halfway across the desk. The springs in his chair shriek like he's a much heavier man.

"Look it," he says. "It's very simple. Do your work. Keep the peace. Respect your elders."

Julian clenches his teeth. "But I've seen that movie a thousand times," he says. "I've answered the same questions over and over, when things are actually getting a lot worse out there." He swings an arm, as if he means the hallways of their own school, the town, the acres and acres of forest around them. "When do we move to the next level?"

"The next level?"

Julian stares into Mr. Neville's confused face. He thinks for a second about opening up, but the words will come out garbled, like an ancient language, nearly foreign. He will not be understood, he knows that already. A desire spikes in him—to talk to his grandfather, to drift in the boat on a chilly evening, staring up at the stars, his grandfather pointing out the Pleiades. Quickly, the impossible craving is followed by a rising agony that he muscles away, picturing Coreen instead, her black-and-pink hair curtained around her face, that bruise, how she would understand. How she'd get it, get him.

"Well," says Mr. Neville, crumpling the orange paper. He overhands it into the garbage can across the room and looks at Julian.

"Nice shot," Julian mutters, and instantly feels like he might throw up. Maybe he can get a note to go home. Then he'll walk over to the river, under the bridge where Rollo's older brother sells pot at lunch hour.

"Go be a kid," Mr. Neville says, gesturing at the door.

ONLY ARNIE IS LEFT, slumped in the middle of the row of blue chairs. Julian wants to ask him where Coreen has gone, but Arnie is absorbed in his phone, thumbs jabbing. His face is slack, and he doesn't see Julian pass by. Maybe I'm the zombie, Julian thinks. Living dead, dragging around this terrible hunger, this emptiness he doesn't understand.

He forgets that the period has changed, that he actually has geography. He goes back to the biology room and finds a different class, the same sub, the same film showing on the screen. The sub is at the desk, writing, her phone staring up at her from the notebook, and she doesn't look up as he walks to the back of the classroom. He finds a seat in the swath of green light spreading from the aquarium. He presses his fingers against the murky glass, watches the red-and-black tetras flicker through the water, a drift of soft green algae that should be scooped out. Most of the other students are staring into their laps or sleeping. No one looks at him. It's like he doesn't even exist.

Point of Ignition

The family lived without love; that much Lonnie could see. Through the fogged solarium window, Howard was a faraway smudge of red in his down vest, chopping wood behind the wreckage of the vegetable garden. Lonnie counted four tomato cages, half toppled, their green metal footings frozen into the earth. They still held fruit, spotted with the same black rot she'd been trying to cut away. One fist was wrapped around her cut finger. Gail glanced at her. "It's all right?"

"I'll live," said Lonnie, uncurling her hand to see a fine line sprouting blood. She felt a sting as the Kleenex pulled away, leaving flakes of tissue stuck to the wound.

"It's over at four-thirty?" Dan asked, entering the kitchen. He handed a plastic bandage to Lonnie. Gail was staring out the window above the sink, turning the handle of the salad spinner, her elbow lifted awkwardly, like an injured wing. There was nothing to see outside but the close wall of the garage.

"Mom," Dan said.

The spinning stopped. "That's what Johnny told me."

There was a chill in the room. Dan's father often turned the furnace off. He wanted to heat the house entirely with wood, but there were too many rooms, most of them separated from each other by walls and narrow doorways. Lonnie would open it right up. Make the dining room and front living room all one big area. Knock out the kitchen wall. If it was her house.

"Are you coming?" Dan asked her. The car keys hung from his fingers.

Lonnie threw out the stained Kleenex and the wrapper from the bandage. It was the cheap kind, and she could already feel the adhesive starting to slip. "I thought we were walking."

Dan looked at his mother. She'd set aside the lettuce and was washing the knife Lonnie had been using. The tomatoes sat, neatly wedged, their glutinous innards clotted with yellow seeds, the black bits pushed to the side.

"There's time," Gail said.

"I could use the walk," Lonnie said. "I mean, the fresh air."

Dan hung the keys on a brass pineapple fixed to the side of the cupboard.

THE TREES HAD BEEN full of leaves when the first snow hit a week earlier. Most hadn't even had a chance to change. They froze and fell in icy green heaps on the front yards. The sun glinted off their crusts.

"My mom likes you," said Dan.

Lonnie took his hand but then let it go. He was wearing gloves with puffy fingers, and she had her thick pink mittens on; it was too difficult to hold on. She didn't know how he could tell about his mother—the two women had barely spoken since she and Dan arrived a few hours earlier, just after lunch. Gail kept remembering things she had to do, settling on the couch, then standing again, putting her rings in a bath of gold cleaner, jotting down a grocery list. Finally, Dan's father had simply left, drifting away so no one noticed he was gone until Gail said she wanted a fire.

"She seems nice," Lonnie told Dan.

"She's been through a lot."

Lonnie met his eye, and it was like a signal for him to look away. His shoes scraped on the sidewalk. He didn't lift his legs when he walked. It annoyed her, that steady shuffling sound like he was reluctant to get anywhere. She looked at the neat houses sided with flagstone and brick, landscaped walkways leading up to their glossy front doors. The day so bright it made her head ache. "I should have brought my sunglasses," she said.

THE DOORS OF THE CHURCH opened, and a slow crowd drifted out. Men, mostly. One in a blue business suit carrying a foam cup. A woman wearing a belted black jacket and jeans with red patches on the knees. She came out with her sunglasses already on and quickly lit a cigarette.

Dan and Lonnie stood on the other side of the road. Cars passed between them and the church. When a clear spot came,

Lonnie moved to cross, but Dan stopped her. He lifted his arm to wave, and Lonnie followed his gaze and saw another Dan, standing on the cement steps. It was as if they were in a reflection, only there wasn't another Lonnie.

The other Dan ran across the busy street. His eyes shone, similar but different from Dan's, Lonnie saw, as Johnny reached out both arms. Dan extended his hand instead, and Lonnie thought the corners of his mouth were forced up or else he was trying not to smile.

"Lonnie," Dan said. "My brother, Johnny."

Johnny grinned. "Lonnie and Johnny," he said.

Dan crossed his arms, rocked back on the heels of his hiking boots as Johnny extended his hand. Lonnie took her mitten off and grasped his chilly palm. Up close, he looked like a slightly chubbier version of Dan. Fuller in the face, his head shaved. He also seemed happier, which surprised Lonnie. She had expected something else. A darker version of Dan: steely but battered.

"Nice to meet you," said Lonnie. She didn't know what else to say.

Johnny nodded, then turned to wave at the woman in sunglasses. He burrowed his fisted hands into the pockets of his leather jacket.

"Who's that?" Dan asked, as the woman threw her butt into a sewer grate and walked in the opposite direction. Her long blond hair shone against her black coat.

"Nobody," said Johnny, then shook his head. "Lisa. We'll see." And he laughed, a single loud guffaw that startled Lonnie after the quiet afternoon.

DAN HAD TOLD Lonnie about his brother on their second date. Over dessert, key lime pie and milky sweet coffee at the fancy restaurant in the Water's Edge Hotel. He described that hitting-bottom moment when Johnny visited Dan for Bacchus. On the way up to the music festival, Johnny said he saw camels and spent the rest of the afternoon hiding in a clutch of cedars on the riverbank. He was high on acid. Eventually Dan just walked away. Every time he told her the story, Dan added new details about Johnny's behaviour. How he screamed at the female bus driver. Kicked mud in Dan's face. But Lonnie found herself thinking about Johnny, too. Ending up alone. Trying to find shelter in the cold night. She didn't ever say anything. Nodded her head like it was on a spring. Stroked Dan's arm as he talked, his voice a squeaky gear.

ON THE WAY HOME, Dan took off his glove and held her hand. They didn't talk until they reached the convenience store and Johnny said he wanted to go inside.

"It'll be supper when we get home," Dan said.

Johnny stood, counting a pile of silver change dredged out of his pocket. Lonnie felt a crackle coming off him. Dan stared at his brother's downturned face and said, "Mom's been cooking half the day."

Johnny looked up. The coins glinted like shattered glass.

"It's lasagna," Lonnie said. Dan's hand in hers felt like a weight.

Johnny's eyes floated over to her but didn't connect. He dropped the coins into his pocket. "Yeah," he said, as if he'd already known, and they continued down the street.

When they got back, Gail was setting the table. They came in the side door, into the kitchen, and heard her through the wall—china clunking, the clatter of cutlery against the hard wood. Howard appeared at the top of the basement stairs, his hair slicked back, wet from the basement shower, and stopped when he saw them.

"Johnny," he said, like a statement of fact, and Johnny reached an arm out to greet him even though he was living there.

As the two men shook hands, Lonnie felt the air shift, like a belt loosened. Howard went into the back room, the den, and soon they heard the crackle of a fire.

"Supper!" Gail shouted, and Lonnie realized she knew they were back.

WINE WASN'T SERVED at dinner even though stemware had been set out. Gail put Johnny at the head of the table, in the only chair with arms. His leg jumped. Lonnie sat to his left and felt it through most of the meal, the steady, rattling lurch. In the kitchen, Gail dished the lasagna onto plates, and Lonnie carried them into the dining room as the men sat back, waiting. She thought of saying something but decided not to. Nobody was noticing, not even Dan, who always offered to help at her mother's house. It seemed the three of them were elsewhere, gazing at separate patches of the glossy mahogany table, focused intently on their own details. Howard cleaned his fingernails with a pocket knife until he saw Lonnie looking and folded the blade back into its red body. Johnny tapped his fingers against the table's edge while Dan spun his napkin ring in the empty space where his plate would go. The brothers were like a band, a duo, working toward a new musical sound. When she slipped Dan's meal in front of him, he turned his face to her and said, "You're the best."

"Your mother made it," Lonnie said, as she and Gail sat down.

Johnny lifted his wineglass, filled with cloudy water just poured from the tap. A few drops ran down the side. "Cheers."

"Johnny," said Howard.

"What?" said Johnny, but Howard just shook his head, his eyes settled on something in the centre of the table. The dried roses in a cut-glass bowl.

Gail picked up the salad and handed it to Johnny. It hovered there, near his face. He didn't move, and she said, "You need greens."

"I'm fine."

She put the bowl down and her fingers crawled across the table toward him, but Johnny pulled his hand away as if touched by a spider. "Well, pass it then," Gail said.

"What about grace?" said Johnny.

Gail looked at Howard. He had already picked up his fork, but he put it down again. He curled his fingers over the edge of the table like he was ready to stand up.

Johnny bowed his head. "Higher power," he said, and paused.

In the sudden absence of sound, Lonnie heard Dan's parents breathing. A low wheeze from Gail, recovering from a cold, and Howard, who let out a long, even exhale. Dan was silent, like his breath was held.

"Thank you for this opportunity," Johnny said. "This meal, and for bringing this stranger into our midst..." His voice faded away like he was telling a story he'd grown tired of.

Lonnie felt her eyelids jumping.

"Amen," he said abruptly, and Gail repeated the word and laid a napkin on her lap. Johnny lifted his fork and started eating, shovelling the next bite into his mouth before he even swallowed.

"She isn't a stranger," Dan said.

"Dan," said Howard.

Lonnie could hear the strain in his voice, as if he wasn't used to talking, although when she'd first arrived, he asked her what her major was, what classes she was taking.

Dan turned to his father. "Well, she isn't."

"She is to us," Johnny said, through the food in his mouth. "Fuck, you are, too."

Gail cringed but didn't speak. Howard's fork hit his plate and he glared down the table at Johnny, who didn't even seem to notice, just kept eating. Lonnie thought he had an invisible shield around him that only allowed things out. His food was already half gone while the others had barely started, including Lonnie, whose cut finger rubbed painfully against the silver handle of her fork.

"She's my girlfriend," Dan said, and it was the first time Lonnie had heard him call her that. Under the table, his cupped hand held her knee, rubbing the hard disc of bone through her jeans, his thumb circling and circling. She asked about salad dressing. Gail wiped her mouth and stood.

"I can get it," Lonnie said, but Gail shook her head and turned toward the kitchen. A log shifted in the wood stove. Lonnie ate the green leaves of the salad and the sweet tomato chunks, the hint of rot a subtle, ugly flavour she could still discern, even with the ranch dressing. She wondered if the others could, too.

LONNIE WAS IN CRISIS when she met Dan. That's what her counsellor called it. Midway through first year she'd gone to the bar where they sold aluminum trays of twenty half-pints for fifteen bucks and gotten drunk with her roommate. Other people were there. People they knew from classes, from school. A blurry face over her when she rose into consciousness. A body fucking hers. She did not struggle, only sank, fell back into a sticky, dragging darkness that went on and on, like getting lost in a swamp. In the morning, even the light seemed different, a tenuous watery grey, when she exited his apartment, tried to figure out where she was.

Ten months later, Dan asked her out after their class on modern Europe. Reluctantly, she agreed, hesitant because of how she'd changed, how he seemed so nice.

AFTER DINNER, Gail put a pot of coffee on. Howard went downstairs to watch television in the room Lonnie was to sleep in, and Gail followed, hastily, because their show had already started. Johnny, Dan, and Lonnie took their coffee into the den.

"Still a stick up his ass," Johnny said. He pinched the couch cushion's rounded edge. Lonnie sat on the floor, bare feet stretched toward the fire. Socks piled beside her.

"He's doing the best he can," Dan said, but Johnny ignored him.

"You're in school?" he asked Lonnie. She twisted around to face him, sat cross-legged.

"Yeah," said Dan, sitting in a brown leather recliner, a cross-hatching of white on the worn arms.

"Poli-sci," she said. "Same as Dan."

"So you'll be prime minister someday."

"I'd rather join the foreign service."

"What's that?"

"You get government posts around the world," she said. "Live in different countries."

She was about to say more, about the exam they'd have to write, the difficulty of it, but Johnny cut her off. "Is that what *you* want to do?" he asked his brother.

Dan didn't answer. He stood and went to the fire and crouched down to prod the end of a log through the open doors. With the iron poker, he pushed it deeper into the flames. It was what he wanted to do. They talked about it all the time.

"First I heard of it," Johnny said. His leg stopped shaking as he leaned forward to lift the mug to his face. Some of the coffee spilled down his chin. He jabbed at his face with the back of his hand to wipe it away. "Drinking problem," he joked.

Dan knocked bits of black charcoal into the flames.

"Dad was here, he'd stop you doing that," Johnny said.

"Dad's not here."

Lonnie drank her coffee.

"How'd you guys meet?" Johnny asked.

They looked at each other. Lonnie felt a prickle in the corners of her mouth, but Dan's face was serious.

"In class," he said. And to Lonnie: "We should go."

"Where are you going?" Johnny asked.

"To see a band," Dan said, as he rose and replaced the poker in its iron stand.

Johnny took another drink, a gulp. Lonnie saw him swallow, the bob of his Adam's apple under the stubbled skin of his throat. She poked her toes into the bulb of a sock.

"We're going to be late," said Dan.

"You'd just fuck off like that," Johnny said. "Just ditch your family."

Lonnie thought he was talking about the band, but Dan said, "That decision's a long way away."

"Still," Johnny said. His eyes flickered orange, reflecting the fire.

Dan shut the doors of the wood stove.

"We're only in second year," said Lonnie.

"We're going to be late," Dan said again.

"Can I come?" Johnny said, and laughed.

"Sure," said Lonnie. She didn't look at Dan.

Johnny blinked, sat upright, guzzled down the rest of his coffee. They both stood at the same time.

ON THEIR FIRST DATE, Dan brought her flowers. She wasn't used to that. When she yelled for him to come in, he stepped inside the small space at the bottom of the stairs that led up to her second-floor apartment. She saw his black Doc Martens shoes and a giant bouquet of yellow and white daisies before he reached the top of the steps and she saw all of him. He was grinning. She felt sick, scared, as he kissed her on the cheek, a dry, courteous press of his lips like nothing she was used to. Since that night in first year, she'd been on only a few dates, if you could call them that. Usually, she drank too much and guided the evening to a place where they'd end up fucking.

"Repeating the trauma," her counsellor suggested, but that annoyed Lonnie.

"Just fucking," she said, and wished she hadn't even mentioned it. She didn't have a vase, so she filled the kitchen sink halfway and leaned Dan's flowers against the tap.

THE BAND WASN'T very good. Johnny, Dan, and Lonnie spent more time driving downtown and back and finding parking than in the bar. The brothers hardly talked. It was her banter that filled the silence and her judgment of the music that made them leave, Dan downing the last of his beer and Johnny pushing aside his ginger ale. Dan said he was tired, anyway. He'd gotten up at six that morning for lacrosse practice before they drove the three hours to his parents'.

At the house, almost all the lights were out. Gail had set out four boxes of cereal and three bowls on the kitchen table. Lonnie stared at it, confused, before Dan told her, "It's for the morning." It was something that never would have happened at her mother's house. Johnny opened the fridge and pulled out a plastic-wrapped plate of lasagna. "That might be for lunch," Dan said, but Johnny lifted a corner, took a large bite, and left it on the counter when he went upstairs.

Lonnie wasn't tired. She had a lot of reading to catch up on and an assignment due on Wednesday. Dan filled a glass of water at the tap. He was supposed to sleep upstairs, in his own room, but they weren't bothering with that. "I'll be down in a minute," she said.

"Don't be long."

It sounded like an order. She was about to speak, to tell him, in a joking way, he wasn't the boss of her, but she noticed the strain on his face. All the lines that would emerge when he was old, already sketched in. She kissed him on the mouth. His lips were wet from the water.

"I won't," she said. And again: "I won't."

THERE WERE RED coals in the stove. Lonnie added a log and sat on the hard edge of the brick hearth, waiting for the fire to reignite. She yawned, pressing her fingers against her wide mouth. Johnny was standing in the doorway when she opened her eyes, a glass of amber liquid in one hand, the lasagna in the other. He came into the room.

"Bedtime reading?" he said, nodding down at the textbook on the floor beside her: *The Balance of Power*.

"Yeah," she said, and gestured to the fire, sluggish but beginning slowly to burn. "I love this."

The tumbler knocked on the coffee table as Johnny set it down. "Apple juice," he said.

HOW IT HAPPENED was this: dates that started out okay but turned into a blur. A biology student who showed her his vermiculture composting system, worms in a box of dirt in the basement, before they left for dinner. Nicely dressed, he opened the car door for her and set his fingers on the small of her back as they followed the hostess to their table. She had on a dirty jean jacket and needed to comb her hair. Too much red wine, and by the time he got her back to his apartment she was sobbing, her nose running snot, and, after, she was sick in his car as he drove her to her place. Then, the bouncer from a bar she and her house-mate went to. A blackout. Waking, shirt off, alone on his living room floor, a sticky memory of giving him head in an alley. After those two, one week apart, she started seeing her counsellor.

JOHNNY LIT A CIGARETTE. "Don't tell," he said, and she hesitated but then reached over the coffee table for a drag. She wanted a drink, could feel the slither of need in her. He got up and opened the glass door to the patio, and when he came back he lifted the poker, pushed the wood around. Flames wove up from the middle, their roots blue. "You have to let it breathe," he said, and she shifted away, gave him access to the stove. Lonnie moved to the chair Dan had been in earlier and swung her legs over the wide arm, trying to look relaxed. She kept glancing over, at the dark patch that was the door into the dining room, where Dan had shown her the collection of family photos on the wall: his high school graduation, Johnny as a baby, the black-and-white snapshot of his parents' wedding day. Her own parents were divorced; she hardly ever saw her dad. Johnny set his smoke on a seam of mortar and shoved a huge, fat log onto the fire, so big that at first she thought it wouldn't fit.

"Dan tell you about me?" he asked.

For a moment, she thought she should lie. "Yeah."

Johnny snorted. He tried to shut the stove door, but a corner of the log kept it open. "Well, Bacchus wasn't the fucking bottom," he said, and she looked down at the cigarette, its orange ember hovering over the carpet, growing ash.

JOHNNY TOLD HER he was already drunk when the guy in Dan's residence slipped him a hit of acid. He'd never done it before. He rode the bus with Dan and his friends until he saw the camels, then someone pulled the cord and Johnny stumbled off when he saw his chance. Dan followed, because he thought he had to, Johnny said. It was a zoo. Johnny wandered the fence, looking in through the chain-link. He found his way down to the river, went swimming. Dan was pissed off, shouting at him, the words electric, burning spirals, while the rocks in the river turned to skulls. "So I hid in the cedars," he said. "Eventually I left, found a bar. In the morning, I hitched home, stole Gail's credit card, bought a ticket to Thunder Bay."

"Why there?"

Johnny shrugged. "Somebody told me about it. Tree-planting work."

He laughed, the same single burst as when they'd first met. At dinner she'd realized the difference between his eyes and Dan's. Johnny's were deep brown where Dan's tended to hazel.

She knew there were details that Johnny had left out. "How's AA?" she asked.

Johnny shrugged. Lonnie realized she was sitting with her knees drawn up, her arms tightly crossed. She pulled her hands off each elbow, curled her feet under her, opened uneasily. Johnny watched her. "Dan's had bad luck with women," he said.

She didn't speak.

"But there's something different about you."

His leg was jumping, and she wanted to reach out, rest her fingertips on his knee, stop the constant quaking, but she couldn't move. Her mouth felt very dry.

"I should go to bed," she said. She got up and went into the kitchen, leaving her book by the fire. At the sink, she guzzled a glass of water and felt Johnny come up behind her. He stepped close, then closer, and she stayed but didn't turn around. In the black window she could see their reflections, double-layered, one shifted slightly off the other as if they each had two bodies. His hand lifted. She skittered sideways, ran down the basement stairs.

"IT'S LIKE I'M TESTING them," she said to her counsellor, a soggy wad of tissue clenched in her fist. All that ugly pain bubbling to the surface like swamp gas. "Just to see what they'll do." The third date, with Dan, followed the same pattern. They went to a movie and then she suggested drinks. A few hours later she passed out beside the toilet, wine-red vomit splattered up under the rim. When she rose, shakily, she found him on her couch. Her jacket stretched over his chest, his shoes still on. It was dawn by then, that fragile, pearlescent light settling against the big bay window, and she made coffee and woke him. When she told him what had happened to her, his hands clenched into fists as the words leaked slowly from her mouth, and she cried and cried.

THERE WAS NO mirror in the rec room, where Dan and Lonnie had slept on the pullout couch. Lonnie had to go to the bathroom to see how she looked. She hadn't slept well. A dream about a stray cat, fighting its way out of her arms, scratching her, had woken her and she'd worried about the fire, if she should have closed the doors of the stove or made sure Johnny had. Dan's side of the bed was empty when she woke, and in the bathroom she saw how grey shadows stained the skin under her eyes. She sat on the toilet, picked at the bandage on her finger, a second one, which had surprisingly stuck through the night.

In the kitchen, Johnny was eating cereal while his mother unloaded the dishwasher.

"Good morning," Lonnie said.

"Morning," said Gail, and she poured her a cup of coffee from the thermos carafe. "Milk's there," she said, pointing to a small yellow jug on the table. Lonnie took sugar also, but there were only pink packets of sweetener. She didn't say anything.

The chair was freezing cold when she sat down. Dan was outside, chopping wood with his father. Johnny stared into his breakfast, fishing bits out of the bowl until he knocked the spoon on the table to show her. Cereal letters spelled out LONNY. After she saw it, he smiled and ate them one by one, but she didn't meet his eyes.

DAN TOLD HIS PARENTS he'd forgotten about an essay that was due, and they left later that morning. "I can't stay any longer," he told Lonnie. Panic in his voice. Johnny was at a meeting.

A light snow drifted down as they drove east on the high-way. They were out of his parents' suburb, the rest of the city behind them, when he asked, "Did he get to you?"

Lonnie looked at him, then reached out to lay a hand on the back of his neck. He thrust his body forward to knock it away.

"Did he tell you his sad stories?"

She didn't know what to say. Outside, the lake was visible beyond the fields.

"Because he does that," Dan said. "He likes to do that."

"We just talked," she finally said.

He was quiet for a long time. It seemed like he was sifting through some sort of rubble, looking for a central point. His face was clenched and red, and she wondered if he would start to cry.

"He's nearly destroyed my parents."

"They seem okay."

"What the fuck do you know?"

Spittle formed on his bottom lip as he told her again about the guy's teeth, broken on the railing in Thunder Bay. The fire Johnny set at the bar. Fifteen thousand dollars' worth of property damage.

Lonnie said nothing. The windshield was fogged from the heat of Dan's breath, so he cracked a window. Cold air gushed into the car, and Dan adjusted the controls, blasting the fan, as Lonnie watched the passing landscape. Farms gave way to a wet-land full of criss-crossed cedar trunks, toppled and silver. Dry tinder as far as the eye could see.

The Great and Powerful

When I was a child, Daddy made me and the other kids kill the chickens. It was to toughen us up, and now I am anything but squeamish. Once I finished, I would go inside, my mind on other things, and one of the mothers would holler at me to take off my dirty boots and shirt. They kept an immaculate house, dust lifted off every surface, the oak railing polished with a beeswax cream.

In university, during the one and a half years I pursued an undergraduate degree—allowed to go on the condition that I study something useful, like botany—a school counsellor told me she thought my family put too much pressure on me. She meant, I think, with the expectation that I be so diligent in the barnyard, helping shovel and spread the manure in the garden soil, overseeing the animals' biological processes of eating, evacuating, and finally being sent to slaughter, but that was how it was for everyone.

"Does that make it all right?" she asked.

I didn't answer. A humming started up in my head, and pretty soon all I saw was her mouth moving, saying my made-up name, prodding me to talk. The walls beyond her head were bumpy concrete. On one, she'd hung a bright South American blanket, probably bought from a travelling merchant in the library foyer. I sat there, lost in the blue-and-fuchsia weave, wanting to get up close and smell it, imagining the earthy, goat-like aroma of the woven wool, the scratchy feel of an animal's hide against the prickly flush of my cheek.

THE DAY WAS ONE of the first warm ones, so my best friend, Heather, and I found a table on the patio at Bohemian Village, in the late-afternoon sunshine. She tapped her silver lighter on the table's wooden surface, which was scarred with deeply carved letters and angular hearts.

"He isn't exactly homeless," I told her, as she swivelled her head to look for the server, lips pursed like a morning glory facing the night. "He's squatting," I said. "That old hat factory on Cherry? The one in the paper last week? With all the rich neighbours complaining?"

Everything was a question because I was looking for agreement, acknowledgement, at least a slight nod. Heather moved her fingers in the air like a piano player warming up, and the waitress walked over. I didn't want beer, but instead of arguing, I slid one of her cigarettes out of its foil envelope and held it to my lips.

"Honey," she said, as she lit it for me. When I drew in air, the tip crackled and glowed. "You know it isn't that. I just think he might be—"

"Did you see Mrs. Johansen's pants today?" I asked. "Those plaid bell-bottoms with the purple clogs?" I stuck a finger in my mouth and pretended to gag at the outfit worn by one of our customers at the market. Even I knew it was out of style, even I, who had until recently never heard of Uggs or True Religion or Britney Spears or a hundred other stars in the wide constellation of capitalism.

"Using you," Heather said. She stared at me, waiting for me to agree with the assessment she'd given of Anders, my boyfriend.

I shook my head. "He has a different lifestyle," I blurted with a puff of smoke. "He doesn't care about one day buying a fancy car or making sure he's in his cubicle on time." An attitude I was used to, an alternative path.

Heather snorted, said nothing else, so neither did I. When our pitcher arrived, she set our glasses side by side and poured. I looked around the patio at the other pockets of smokers, all of us in our own separate pods. It reminded me of *Blade Runner*, those floating cars flinging past one another in the caverns between skyscrapers, which I'd seen for the first time the week before, when Anders had commented on the poster outside the Revue Cinema. I had paid for the tickets, hands trembling. Movies were still so new and alarming, and I could hear Daddy saying how they stole your faculties, hypnotized you to pulp. I felt like pulp, and if Heather really cared, I would have spread myself out on the table between us, letting out my giddiness, telling her again about the lightning bolt of sudden attraction that had hit Anders and me. I'd fallen in love. But my joy stayed buried beneath her obvious opinion and the voice in my head of Mother Lila, the sarcastic one, caustic as she judged me: A homeless man? I guess it'll be an outdoor wedding.

THAT NIGHT, ON THE WALK back to my rented room, I peed in a garage-lined laneway. Sometimes I did that. Dropped my jeans and underwear beside a row of dented aluminum garbage cans, squatted, and stared up at the moon as urine splashed to the ground. It wasn't just a drunk thing. I did it to feel connected to the earth. Because in a lot of ways I still missed home, where the rhubarb harvest would soon be starting, where the air would be dense with pungent aromas. Anders would approve, I thought, and bit my bottom lip, wondering again if I could bring him home, if we could together cross that smouldering bridge.

When I told him about this habit the next afternoon, he paused thoughtfully before asking, "What do you do if you have to take a shit?" We were sitting on a park bench, holding foam cups with plastic lids. My face burned red. When I didn't answer, he said, "It's just another part of the reality."

"I know," I said, but in truth I felt uneasy. What did I know about reality? I could barely understand the disposable cup I was holding—one use and then you toss it? Where did it go? Who had made the plastic lid? I pictured workers toiling in a large, dark factory that looked like the images of the future that Daddy painted on large canvasses, sold to tourists for thousands of quid, which was what Anders called money.

He rubbed at a deep crack in the sidewalk with the sole of his black dress shoe, back and forth over the mud-stuffed gap. I chewed on the edge of the cup until a hunk broke off, mouth-shaped, then I spit it onto the ground.

"Do you have any cigarettes?" he asked. I only ever smoked Heather's, so we walked to the 7-Eleven, where I paid for a blue-and-white pack of Belmont Milds. "Ta," he mumbled when I handed it to him, and that worried me because of what Heather had said. He wasn't using me; this wasn't charity or a donation to the needy. That wasn't what I wanted at all. I was tired of that feeling, like I—and all the other members of the Community—was better than every other human in the crowded outside world.

After we left the store, we headed for a picnic table in the park. The grass was wet and water soaked through my canvas shoes and red stockings and I hopped back and forth. Anders laughed at me, but not like I was a spoiled baby, like I'd never slept outside in a blizzard, like I didn't know how hunger felt, like my suffering didn't match his. I looked like an idiot, I knew, so I laughed, too.

Through the smoke of his cigarette, Anders squinted at me. "I'm not a loser, you know," he said, dark eyes accusing. "I used to run mountain rambles. I was the leader, like."

I nodded and touched his elbow, let my fingers creep around to grip the boniness of his wrist. He pulled away, but only to lift his arm and wrap it around me, and I shuffled closer to his meagre warmth. He looked down at my wet feet. They were freezing, the thin white fabric of my shoes stained with soot and grass streaks from last summer, completely inappropriate for the weather but all I had. I tucked them under the table.

"Now people are always thinking I don't belong."

I reached for his hand, the one holding the cigarette. "I don't think that."

His knee bobbed up and down, but his fingers didn't move. They just sat there, under mine, waxy and cold in the early-spring sun, and we both watched his smoke burn down, the ember dulled to a pillar of ash.

ANDERS GREW UP in a city, the capital of Wales, called Cardiff. When he was seventeen, he started shooting heroin with his best friend's sister, and after she died from an overdose he went in and out of rehab until he realized he had to just leave. He travelled, went to work on a freighter carrying olives from Greece, ended up in Montreal, then hitched to Toronto. His father was a coal miner, and his grandfather before him, but he couldn't go underground. Down there in that blackness, he said, a far-off look in his face as he gazed toward the edge of the park. I loved listening to him, how his accent made it sound like he was singing when he spoke, but sometimes he talked really fast and I couldn't understand. My eyelids would flutter open as I strained to hear or else asked him to repeat himself. The space between us like a choppy sea I felt compelled to cross.

"YOU WERE HIGH," Heather said at work a couple days after our drinks at the Bohemian. It had gotten cold again. Jamal, the ukulele player who busked our corner, had a sleeping bag hung over his shoulders with a long gash spitting out stuffing.

Methodically, I pulled yellow and orange peppers out of a cardboard box. I laid them side by side on the fake green grass lining the wooden shelves.

"So?" Her cheeks were flushed but her lips were pale. She didn't look well. "So how do you know how you really felt?"

She meant at the protest where I'd first met Anders. Chants shouted at the cops lined up in front of the embassy, holding scratched Plexiglas shields in front of their stern faces, a scene probably similar to where my mother had first met Daddy and his congregants, joined the circle watching him as he preached from atop his velvet-lined box, just outside the fray. I watched, eyes wide, until my friend Bobby tugged me inside the dark mouth of an alley beside a Thai grocer to smoke a joint. When we heard a clanging beside us, we turned to see Anders climbing out of a Dumpster.

"Hey!" Bobby said, and put a hand over his mouth. He was like that, paranoid, always loud about it. Plus Anders had interrupted his long lecture on media and the culture of image that I wasn't even listening to, that had been moving along like the hum of insects in the garden in June while I stared across the road at the embassy's ten-foot-tall iron doors, wondering if people actually opened and closed them to slip out for a smoke break or a bag of potato chips in the afternoon. It looked like the entrance to a palace, and that voice boomed in my head—*I am the great and powerful*—or whatever those words were from *The Wizard of Oz*, the first film I saw after I left the Community, when I watched wide-eyed as the flat black-and-white world turned to vivid colour.

Anders walked toward us, carrying a clutch of carrots, their long pale roots tangled together. In his other hand, he held out an apple with green-and-red hemispheres. When my eyes met his, I had this sense that I knew him, that we'd met before. *There you are*, I thought, and reached for the apple, as if enchanted.

Bobby said, "You're not going to eat that, are you? It just came out of—"

I took a big bite, holding Anders's gaze until I gagged on soft rot, spat up the chunk. He stared at me, mouth slightly open. The smell of garbage was in my face.

Anders pressed his knuckles against his lips, his eyes lit.

I WALKED HIM BACK to his squat, down a long alley lined with ochre brick, more metal Dumpsters. The cracked asphalt sank under rainbow-skinned puddles outlined in grimy froth. I reached out to hold Anders's hand and his skin felt cold in his unravelling, fingerless gloves. "Shit," he said, but he didn't let go. I'm just like that, I guess. When I see something I want, I go for it, no matter how hard the journey. And back then it mattered even more because I felt like a puppet with its strings slashed, like the scarecrow with his stuffing knocked out. Before I left Anders that day, I gave him a five-dollar bill and he kissed me gently on the cheek. All the way to the streetcar stop, I focused on the warm imprint of his lips until I imagined that people could see it: throbbing on my thin skin, slowly melting into my mouth.

I CUPPED a green pepper that had grown strangely, curled top to end. "It was love at first sight," I told Heather, staring at the odd fruit. Our boss had asked us to segregate the weirdest ones, the ones people wouldn't buy, and put them in the free bin on the stand outside the store, but I liked to give every one of them a chance.

"I'm not sure you're okay," Heather said.

"Sometimes you just recognize things. People, I mean," I told her, still hoping she'd understand. "It's like fate."

"How much money have you given him?" she asked.

"He's my partner."

Her mouth fell open. I put the pepper down and picked up a group of mushrooms that had tumbled to the ground.

"He's homeless," Heather said. "How does he even clean—"

"He showers once a week." My voice rose as I added, "And he's squatting," annoyed at having to explain his living situation once again. "You're just jealous."

She bugged her eyes out at me. "Seriously?"

"I'm sorry it didn't work out for you."

Alex, we were both thinking. The one-night stand with the musician who was married, his wife and baby back in Kentucky. How she obsessed about him for weeks, flinging out emails that were never answered.

Her hand churned through the loose change in the pocket of her floral-patterned apron. "That was totally different."

"Why?" I asked.

"Because it is," she said.

I moved on to the Scotch bonnets, setting aside any with obvious bruises. I had to wear latex gloves, the kind doctors use, because the peppers were so hot.

When I didn't speak again, she threw her arms up in the air. "You're fucking insane," she said, and turned back to repricing the arugula.

"Sometimes you just know," I shouted. It's what my mother had once told me—when I was little, when she hadn't yet disappeared—about her very first sighting of Daddy. Startled at my sudden outburst, a customer looked up from shovelling lychee nuts into a bag. Behind him, through the thick plastic windows, a blur of wet snow fell to the ground.

"ONCE, I WAS AN EXTRA in a film and the director asked me if I'd consider it as a profession," Anders told me, as we squeezed along a chain-link fence to the back of the hat factory. In hindsight, every sign that afternoon was pointing to the end, that this would be the last time I'd see him, but I couldn't tell right then.

"Why don't you?" I asked.

He blinked. I saw the sadness in his eyes, noticed the faint scrawl of crow's feet. I didn't know his age, but he was older than me. "It might be an option," he said, and threw his butt against the brick wall, which was covered in swirling green graffiti tags, the white outline of a leering skull. "But maybe it's time to go home," he said.

My gaze was stuck to the spot where the sparks had flared, then vanished. "Don't go," I said. "Please don't go."

He sighed, slipped an arm around me, pulled me into the spicy, intoxicating power of his scent, like cumin in a warm kitchen full of soft bodies preparing a feast.

I closed my eyes.

"You little bee," he said. It's what he called me, because I buzzed around him, because I stopped to smell the new blooms.

By an apple tree around the back of the factory, boards covering a window had been splintered open. We squeezed through, dropped to the basement floor, and he took me upstairs to his corner, washed yellow from the sun falling through a hole he'd made in the plywood. We lay on a ratty brown Ikea couch scratched to its wooden frame by cats, curled together, dozing in the wide, warm shafts of light.

HEATHER SENT A LETTER. It wasn't hard to find the address. Everyone in the world knew the Community, knew Daddy. He'd even been on *Oprah* once.

She's fallen for a man who lives on the street, Heather wrote. *She seems to be delusional.* Back at home I found the blue-lined loose-leaf, covered in her careful cursive loops. I crumpled it into a hard ball and dropped it down the toilet. What did she know about me, I thought angrily, forgetting she knew all of it, because I'd told her everything. *I don't know what else to do,* she'd written.

Nobody said anything about Anders or my time away, how I'd melted out of the university, then disappeared. How I might have been free if I hadn't trusted someone, if I hadn't opened my big mouth, if I hadn't argued to keep the kind of true love I'd always imagined. It was me who had been stupid, so I took the punishment for my transgressions, then let everything slump back into normalcy, moving gingerly around my sore parts as I helped with the harvest. The first crops of mustard greens were coming up and the strawberries would soon be ready for the tourists who came as much to ogle us as for the sweet fruit. Each morning a pale pink pill appeared beside my tomato juice in a small wooden box that used to hold the children's baby teeth. I let its bitterness seep into my tongue.

My heart was broken, but I didn't complain—about the work or the growing heat of my attic room. When one of the barn cats had kittens, I smuggled the runt inside as soon as her blue eyes opened and named her Apple, like the actress Gwyneth Paltrow's baby, a name you wouldn't know could be a name unless you were totally free. In bed, I held her warm, purring body in the crook of my arm and yearned for Anders, for the sounds and ugliest smells of the city, even for Heather, who sent me a card to say she was sorry, to try to explain her actions, which I found on Mother Lila's desk one day when I was trying to gain access to the powerful, shielded internet to check bus schedules and the cost of a one-way ticket back to the city. I did not respond because I couldn't. My life went back to how it had been. At night, exhausted from the day's work, I struggled to keep my eyes open long enough to kiss Anders goodnight in my mind as I listened to the chirping of frogs in the marsh, eager to find their mates, and past that, farther distant, the coyotes, crazily celebrating a fresh kill.

That Lift of Flight

Hungover, Sarah tries not to stumble on the hillside trail. She's looking down at her notebook, scribbling corrections, clarifying descriptions, writing out what their guide, Tom, said about the hike at the beginning of the dirt path. She can hear him talking up ahead but doesn't notice when he stops, so abruptly that she nearly runs right into him. Her palm presses against his broad, muscular back to avoid a collision, but he doesn't seem to register her touch. Excitedly, he points at a prickly cholla cactus to their right and the eyes of everyone in the group follow his finger. At first, Sarah doesn't see anything. Only creosote shrubs growing out of the pinkish earth, a scattering of red prickly pears rotting on the ground. Then the bird comes clear, perched in the spiky foliage, ruffling its brown-and-white-barred wings.

"A cactus wren," Tom says, eyes sparkling above his T-shirt, emblazoned with *Phoenix Adventures* in orange cursive. He searches the terrain, then strides up the slope to a saguaro cactus with straw bursting out of a hole in its trunk. "The nest."

It's nothing extraordinary; just a dark hole. The others crowd close, pushing into Sarah, trying to lean their camera lenses into the opening.

When the bird lets out a call that sounds like sticks rubbing together, Tom says, "That's a warning."

Sarah moves back, squeezing out of the sweaty crush. She's tired, and aware of how she must look: the slight smear of last night's mascara smudged into the wrinkles around her eyes, tendrils of hair stuck to her sweaty temples. Her knees are aching, too; she's more than ready for the spa part of the press trip.

Ellie had planned to start with that this morning after the two of them drank too many muddled cocktails in the resort's bar the previous night. It was good to see her. It had been ages, not since the fish boil in Wisconsin when Sarah was on the arts track. This time they've traded places. Ellie on arts and crafts, visiting galleries and Frank Lloyd Wright's winter home, while Sarah's covering the outdoor excursions. Up at five, Sarah had already started her day in a crowded hot-air balloon, watching the sun rise over the Superstition Mountains before a breakfast of mimosas and croissants in the desert, while Ellie, she imagined, had been sleeping in, having coffee in her room, before donning the puffy bathrobe to visit the resort's spa.

Her stomach growls. She glances at the schedule, folded into the back of her steno pad. After the hike, they'll eat lunch at the Phoenician. Then, a tour of a 1,500-year-old Hohokam ruin, an art museum, and, finally, the last, fancy dinner, at the

Biltmore. She feels a shiver of excitement, thinking ahead to the evening: the slinky black dress she put on her Visa back home, sparkling costume jewellery, a perfume that smells like orange blossom and ylang-ylang.

And Lucas.

All the way there, on the flight from Toronto to Atlanta, then across to Phoenix, he had been on her mind. Those three other press trips. They took fly-fishing lessons in Michigan, motored out on a lobster boat in Maine, ate too many luscious meals to count and drank too much complimentary wine, all in a blur of a few days each time. There was something about him: his eyes the colour of soot, hair the same colour but going grey at the temples, although he was six years younger than her. A sharp attention, a particular focus. On the last trip, near the Daniel Boone National Forest in Kentucky, there was gossip, Sarah heard, after she invited him to her room in the lodge to drink a bottle of fruit wine that wouldn't fit into her suitcase, which groaned from the weight of press packs and gifts. Others had joined them with their own bottles, but he stayed behind, talking about his ex-wife while Sarah stretched out on the bed, drinking, downing the whole bottle herself. Nothing happened, but it could have.

And he's on this trip, too. Somewhere. She'd seen his name on the press list.

"Do the birds kill the cactus?" someone asks.

Tom shakes his head. "A woodpecker would have made the hole, digging for bugs. It's empty until the birds move in, make a home."

"Sarah," says a voice, and Sarah turns to see Mary, a writer from Boston, sitting on the husk of a dead cactus, beside her husband, Jorge, a photographer who's breathing heavily, hunched over. At first Sarah thinks they need help, but Mary points to the ground, at a square of paper glowing against the sand. One of Martin's notes. It must have fluttered out of her steno pad.

Jorge straightens, both hands holding the large camera in his lap like a baby. "Aren't you going to pick that up?"

TWO DAYS AGO, the drive to the resort: streaks of red and yellow light, shadowy trees full of ripe oranges, tall saguaro cacti lining the medians. They reminded her of outlaws, sturdy yet surrendering, arms up. In the van, she pulled out her notepad to jot the idea down.

"Always working," Alison joked, setting her cellphone into the cup holder, and Sarah hoped she had impressed her with her work ethic because she hasn't yet sold an article, doesn't have an assignment, sat at her desk for hours the week before as wet snow pummelled the windows while she searched for markets to pitch after her usuals declined. She's come to love these press trips: everything paid for, the chance to stay in luxury hotels, eat fine food, enjoy experiences she would never be able to afford. She doesn't want the invitations to stop.

At the hotel, she stepped out of the van's cool air-conditioning into heat scented from the outdoor fires that Sarah would see later from her room. Young men circled the flames, ties loosened, sleeves rolled up, beer glasses glinting.

Their smooth young faces gleamed. The kind of guys Martin had been friends with in university, Sarah thought. Science majors who held keg parties, rowed in teams on the river at dawn, filled shabby student rental houses with their powerful bravado. Never her type. She pulled the curtains closed, and when she opened her suitcase in the welcoming hush of the room, she found the first note.

Don't forget me, it said.

Martin's familiar block print on a square from a sticky pad. Crumpled tightly in her grip, the note fell heavily into the trash can.

This one, the second, is harsher, less needy. More like Martin, actually. *Make your mind up.* She shoves it into the pocket of her capris, a prickling rush of anger spreading under her skin. Mary arches her eyebrows, expectant, as if she has a right to know.

"My husband," Sarah says.

Mary smiles. The rest of the group has moved on. Tom is telling them about creosote, how the root systems survived atomic tests blasts in the fifties. When she turns to follow, Sarah hears Mary whisper to Jorge—"Romance. Remember that?"—as she helps him to his feet.

SARAH MET MARTIN for the first time in university, nearly thirty years ago. They were both in a class on the botany of the boreal region. He sat near the front, serious, jotting notes in a black binder, carefully examining each diagram as it appeared on the screen. Sarah was torn between the arts and the sciences, and it was that class that cinched it for her—how boring it was, the professor's deep monotone putting her regularly to sleep—plus the fact that a play of hers had been chosen for a festival at the student theatre. Martin came to see the play, and afterwards they had drinks. He wanted to be an arborist. They hadn't gotten together then, had drifted their separate ways because Sarah was already sleeping with one of the actors.

Years later, when Sarah was thirty-four, they met again, both back in their university town for the annual rowing regatta, a sort of homecoming. He was divorced, his first wife a lesbian who'd finally come out. They were married ten months later. "He grounds her," Sarah's sister, Ruth, said in a toast at their wedding. As if Martin controls gravity with the weight of a good job, his budgeting skills, his solid common sense. Like that is more important than what Sarah desires: the opening of the world's wide arms, that exhilarating lift of flight.

THERE'S A CHANGE in the schedule. The visit to the prehistoric site has been postponed to the next day, the last day, so they have some free time. Sarah goes to the spa and chooses a treatment that will work well in her article—a salt scrub flavoured with prickly pear and agave—but it stings her skin. Alone in the treatment room, she lies there, tense, counting down the seconds until they'll rinse it off, remembering Israel, the visit to the Dead Sea, the stabbing sensation as she waded into the murky grey water for that classic photograph. Sitting, buoyant, reading a newspaper.

Back in her room, Sarah stands in front of the mirror and examines her skin, flushed red, hoping the angry colour will fade before she puts on her black dress. She eats the chocolate on the pillow and pulls down the comforter, half expecting to find another note, that Martin has called ahead to arrange it, but there's nothing but the perfect spread of the bedsheet. She climbs in, naked. The odour of burning mesquite drifts in from the constant fires, fuelled by natural gas. A waste, Martin would say, a goddamned waste of resources. He hated staying in hotels with her, how she wanted fresh towels every day, how they ate their free buffet breakfasts on disposable plastic dishes at the lower-end places they could afford. He's there with her, in her head, but she turns away, trailing her fingers over the scoured softness of her skin. When the phone rings, screaming into the silence, she wakes with a sharp sense of panic, realizing that too much time has passed, and a sob sputters out before she catches herself, lunges to answer the call.

THE VAN WAITS five minutes. That's the rule. It is frowned upon to miss anything, to be sick, to want to pause. You sign up for the marathon and you run it, so Sarah dresses quickly and rushes down to the lobby, waving to Alison as she bursts out of the elevator. There's no time to grab a coffee, although she longs for one, her mind muddled, her forty-seven-year-old body beginning to falter. She pulls her tangled, sticky hair into a ponytail as she steps out the front door, and there's Lucas, climbing into the back of the other minivan.

"Where are they going?" Sarah asks Ellie, who's sitting in the back of the brown van. Alison is still in the lobby, rounding up the other writers, calling their rooms.

Ellie looks up from marking details with scribbled stars. Her pen hangs over the notebook. In the distance, the other vehicle passes through the resort's pink stone gates. "I think same as us. The museum, then dinner."

"We'll be back to change?" Sarah asks.

"Don't know," says Ellie, who's wearing black yoga pants, a T-shirt, a hoodie embroidered with a tiny red lobster. Sarah has the same one.

"It's the Biltmore!"

"There'll be time," Alison says, sliding behind the wheel. "Somebody come up here so I don't feel like a chauffeur."

Ellie and Sarah glance at each other. "Go on," Ellie says.

Alison's a talker. Sarah's known her for years, since she started doing press trips. As they drive through the resort gates, Sarah asks about Gerry, Alison's long-time fiancé who's the VP of the PR firm.

"He's in Michigan," Alison says. "A gallery tour."

They drive past the golf course, which, according to the press pack, is irrigated with grey water. The gardens are full of cacti and succulents. Sarah would like to slow down, wander the property, sit by the outdoor fires, take the time to write, but there's no time. There's never any time.

Martin hates press trips because of that—the constant rush, the quick sampling of one experience after another. "How can you take anything in?" he asked her once, with a tone of amazement that annoyed her.

"I'm not on vacation," she snapped, wondering what he expected, what fantasy he'd built. The same as everyone else: free travel, lucky her. Not untrue; not the whole story either.

Alison says nothing else, surprising Sarah. The neighbourhood starts to change—slick storefronts turning to broken and boarded-up windows, bright pawn shops—and Sarah asks, "Everything okay?"

"Hunky dory," Alison says, an edge to her voice.

Sarah waits a moment, then turns to watch the city slide by, accidentally meeting the eye of a woman dangling her foot off the sidewalk before the light has changed to red; her face is bony, nearly emaciated, scabs spot her arms. Quickly, Sarah looks away. Early on, she learned not to admit to the reality of a city's poverty, crime, any aspect that might keep people from visiting. In Israel, she once made the mistake of asking a vineyard owner about water, where he got it, and had felt eyes slide and connect all over the room as he evaded the question.

"The Jordan Valley," another journalist, Ron, had told her when they were back on the bus, most of them half tanked from sampling and not spitting. "It's piped from an aquifer in the West Bank," he clarified, leaning over the back of her seat to be heard above the roar of happy conversation. He waited, his eyes heavy with meaning, but what did she have to say to that? She turned away and started writing: *Water is turned expertly into wine in the Golan Heights, where grapes have grown in the dusty soil for millennia. Enjoy samples at an Israeli vineyard operated by the same family since the late 1960s.* She scratched out a few words, switched a couple clauses around, avoided the passive voice. That's her job.

TRAVEL, THE ITCH for it, the wanderlust, came to her early. As a kid she'd escape her arguing parents to stand on the beach up the road from her house and dream about the Indian Ocean, the Mediterranean Sea, the Caribbean. In winter, the vast white platform of the huge lake became the Gobi Desert, horizon blurred by sand instead of snow, her only transport by camel. The ice boomed and creaked, breaking open in the spring, and one summer, when she was seventeen, she went on her own to Ireland to visit a cousin her age whom she had started writing after finding her name on their family tree. She was hooked. The strange currency, the accents, driving on the other side of the road excited her, but what she really loved was the feeling that all around her doors were waiting to be opened. That the normal constrictions had eased. On that trip, she lost her virginity, willingly, ecstatically, her spine pressed into the cold stone floor of a fifteenth-century castle. Back home, she wrote an article for her town newspaper, illustrated with a picture of herself, hair a mess, flushed face lit with joy as she was held upside down to kiss the Blarney Stone.

Martin, in contrast, is a homebody. She knew that; she learned it early on. There was a moment when she knew she shouldn't marry him. That they were too different; they didn't want the same things. She's been thinking about it lately because the marriage counsellor asked them to reflect on what had brought them together, why they'd started dating, what they'd first felt. In her office, Martin had stared at his fingertips, scarred from rough bark and pine needles, and when he looked up, she saw his slight grin, his dewy eyes, while her own mind had turned to an afternoon a week before their wedding. The canoe tipped to one side, pulled up on a ledge of rock. A bottle of wine leaning against a low juniper bush. The warm spring sun had coated her face like oil, and when she said, "Imagine we're in the South of France," he answered, "What's wrong with right here?"

She widened her eyes, surprised at his tone. "You know what I mean."

"Why do you always have to be somewhere else?" he asked, picking apart a green berry.

"I don't," she said sharply, but she wondered now if that was true.

If that was what she really wanted: not sameness, monogamy, but variety, exploration, movement through the possibilities.

Beside him, that day, the clear base of a plastic wineglass had glinted in the sun like a strange coin. They watched a cormorant dive, swim down for fish, and it reminded her of a documentary she'd seen about traditional fishermen in China. The landscape—those sharp jutting mountains, the green terraced gardens—had enticed her. She started to tell him about it, then stopped herself. What he wanted were roots, kids, and for a time—aged thirty-five, thirty-six, thirty-seven, thirty-eight—she'd thought she wanted that, too. It was what you did, wasn't it? Settled down. Made a life.

They tried; for more than four years they tried. Sarah had a vision of her family: a boy and a girl. Taking them to Disney World or the smaller theme park in California. Learning how to sew miniature dresses and tiny tops, taking some time off from the constant hustle of freelancing. Instead she got inner arms spotted with purple bruises when they took blood daily to monitor her hormones, drugs that made her swollen and weepy, IUIS, and the devastating failure of the IVF, which cost them $18,000 on a line of credit they've barely even dented. All for nothing. Her body as silent as an unreachable ocean depth. Deep down, now, she wonders if it's because she didn't really want it.

AT THE MUSEUM, they're given guidebooks and left on their own. The other group, Lucas's, has gone ahead into the exhibits on residential schools and Hopi pottery. Ellie heads for the gift shop to buy a book about kachina dolls, and Sarah passes alone through the arched doorways, into the Spanish-Colonial mansion that houses the main collection. In one room, a huge red bloom by Georgia O'Keeffe draws her close.

"Trying to smell it?" Lucas jokes.

"There you are," she says, turning toward him. She feels her cheeks flush.

He approaches, eyes on hers, then steps close to the painting, lifting a single finger as if to touch the petal's curve.

"Sir," says the guard, stepping out of the corner of the room.

Lucas jerks his hand away and lifts both arms in mock surrender. He steps back and bumps into her. They stand like that, close, the guard watching. Her breath comes quickly. She feels giddy, alive, not unlike when she was young, arriving in a new country, an unexplored city. The first time she went to Prague when she was twenty-one. Rose up and up and up that impossibly high escalator on the subway journey from the airport and emerged in the Old Town and had to sit down, so stunned by the beauty of the place. Lucas's camera swings on his shoulder as he steps away, and Sarah walks with him. Mary nearby, muttering into a tape recorder, watching them as Lucas whispers, "Where've you been, anyway?"

"Around."

"So noncommittal."

She smiles. They wander to the next painting, then the next.

"I got a treatment from George Clooney's masseuse today," he says.

"Anything rub off on you?"

"I hope not."

She laughs. His eyes, dark and bright, flicker over her face.

"Dinner tonight?" he asks.

"Dinner," she repeats, and he nods, then slips away, lifting his camera to photograph a man holding a young girl in his arms in front of a landscape painting. Blue-grey mountains, Native Americans on horseback, a spiral of smoke rising from a fire in the centre of three teepees, the sky lit with pink dusk. It's beautiful, and Sarah writes down its name, the artist's name. When she lifts her head, Lucas has again disappeared.

THE NEXT NOTE is inside the left cup of her bra, the black lace push-up she bought for the trip and hid from Martin. She doesn't read it. She crumples it and throws it at the bathroom wastebasket, where it hits the edge and ricochets under the vanity to settle in a dark corner like mould.

"Fuck," she snaps, but leaves it to get on with things: fastening the bra, scooping her breasts up to fit, dropping the dress over her shoulders so it falls in cool waves around her skin. She smears cover-up under her eyes, scrapes mascara through her lashes, tousles her still-damp hair to get some sort of sexy look. She'd wanted the slow, languorous process of getting ready, rubbing lavender lotion into her skin, anticipating, attempting to ignore the slivers of guilt, but they'd returned to the hotel with only twenty minutes to shower and dress. As she leaves the room, the phone rings, a blurting scream. She pauses, then lets the brass hinges swing the heavy door closed for her and walks away.

SARAH IS OVERDRESSED. The others are wearing cotton sundresses and casual pants, black jackets and jeans. In her stilettos, she towers over almost everyone, especially Ellie, who's much shorter, who gazes up at her in amused shock as they stand side by side on the terrazzo floor.

"Well, we know who can change the light bulbs," she says, but Sarah ignores her, gazing instead at the dish of light that is her martini, the perfect gleam of its olive spear, then up at the ornate gold-leaf ceiling. During the tour—of the turquoise-tiled pool where Marilyn Monroe swam while Arthur Miller sunbathed, of Nancy and Ronald Reagan's honeymoon suite—her eyes float through the crowd, looking for Lucas, but she doesn't see him until they enter the dining room, Ellie holding her arm as they walk the length of a banquet table. She's already tipsy.

"Here," Sarah says, gripping the chair across from him. He glances up from the menu and smiles as Sarah drops into the chair. The waiter, white-jacketed, plucks the napkin off the table to hand it to her. She takes it, then turns to Ellie. "Let's go have a cigarette," she says.

Ellie rolls her eyes. "I quit, remember? Not getting any younger."

The starters come. Bocconcini salad with shredded leaves of basil, olive oil drizzled in pools of gold. Sarah takes small bites until she realizes how hungry she is, then she shovels the food into her mouth, wiping the oil off her bottom lip with her thumb. When she looks up again, Lucas is talking to Alison, who's rushed in from dealing with some problem to join them. She's describing something with her slim hands, holding them parallel, like two walls, then cupping them together. They are naked of any rings, Sarah notices, as Alison's green eyes flicker under the fringe of her honey-blond hair toward Lucas's attention.

Tomorrow, Sarah goes home; they all do. Heaviness fills her, sudden exhaustion. She lifts her empty glass when the server takes Ellie's plate, basil pushed to one side, while Sarah's is cleaned, nearly shiny. As the red wine gushes out of the green bottle, Sarah catches Lucas's eyes on her. He lifts the glass to his mouth, tips it toward her. A tiny, secret toast.

"What's up next for you?" Ellie asks, catching Sarah's attention away. She breathes in to talk, inhales a sharp thread of merlot, and starts coughing, coughs hard into a bunched-up napkin pushed against her mouth. Everyone looks; Ellie's hand on her back, slapping. Sarah's face burns. She shakes her head, pulls away from Ellie, and stands to leave. Body thumping along on the high heels she hardly ever wears. This winter she's put on weight; they pinch her swollen feet.

In the restroom, she leans toward her face in the mirror. Eyes bloodshot, wiry grey strands in her straight auburn hair, lines around her eyes, a mess of wrinkles on her chest. After that last appointment, the one when the counsellor had suggested they find creative ways to communicate, Martin asked her where she thought they stood. It's what he does as an arborist: assesses structures, makes things stable, cuts them down carefully if they are ready to fall. She hadn't known how to answer. All she knew was how unhappy she felt, how bored, how stuck. Like being on a grounded plane when you don't know what's wrong, the interminable waiting of hours on the runway, unable to disembark.

The water from the automatic tap is cool on her hands. She lets it run, presses her palms against her cheeks, sorts her hair. Her head feels thick from the wine.

Outside, Lucas is leaning against the wood panelling across the carpeted hall. Grinning, he holds up two cigarettes. Part of her wants simplicity, to return to the hotel and ease her tired body into bed, but she also feels she's already gone too far, that the choice has been made. That night in Kentucky, that's what had happened. After midnight, sloppily drunk in her hotel room, she leaned over the edge of the precipice, asked him to kiss her. He pushed her back, his hand accidentally grazing her breast. They hung there for a moment, suspended between options at the door of her room, until he was the one who said no. The door clicked emphatically shut, a sound that sent her down into darkness, burying her face in the sterile hotel sheets. Now she steps toward him, her eyes on his, reaching for his offering. Her belly churns. That lift of flight.

SHE'S IN A SWAMP. Silver trees like thorns against the sky. They are trying to pitch a tent—she and Martin and somebody else—but the ground keeps giving way, the water flooding their shoes. While they're sinking, she opens her eyes, and the true, hard details come rushing in. Sharp red numbers on the alarm clock. Yellow glare of the light bulb in the lamp. Crumpled ball of paper on the bedside table.

The room smells of coffee and the sour odour of mesquite that's starting to make her feel sick. She shifts and her dress twists around her legs, binding her. Noises emerge from the bathroom: running water, the rush of the toilet flushing, and she rolls onto her side, feels the dangle of her earrings, remembers. Her loud, stumbling walk out of the Biltmore after the crème brûlée. The look on the face of the local chamber person, lips pursed in annoyance, as she clutched Tom's hard-muscled arm, told him how much she had enjoyed the hike. Then she, Ellie, and Lucas, out at the fires with the businessmen—business boys she'd called them, over and over, laughing, until they left. It's her dress that stinks, she realizes, and remembers Ellie watching as she and Lucas smoked cigarettes, passing the time while they waited for her to leave.

The bathroom door opens. "Good morning," a voice says, over the sound of pouring coffee. It isn't Lucas's velvet tone, sinking into her ear last night, his breath hot against her neck, inviting her up to his room. Ellie sets a mug of coffee on the bedside table, beside Martin's note.

"Thanks," Sarah says.

"You weren't thanking me last night."

"Isn't she an adult?" Lucas had insisted. The two of them squabbling over her like divorced parents. Ellie's voice followed her down the hallway as Sarah kicked off her heels, walked passively to her room. "She's going through a rough patch," she said. "She asked me to look out for her, not let her do anything stupid. Sorry, Luc, but I think this might be stupid."

Had she? Yes. Over that third sixteen-dollar muddled drink in the resort bar, she'd told Ellie about Martin's note, expecting her to echo Sarah's irritation.

"It's a kind of control," Sarah had said. "You know?"

"Is it?" Ellie asked, like the marriage counsellor might have, and Sarah had started talking. In the hallway, outside her room, she felt a flood of regret, knowing it was too late. She would never see Lucas again. Not like that. Not at night, around a desert fire, carefree, or so she'd felt. Desired and desiring.

Living for the moment.

Free.

That's not freedom, Martin says in her head. What he'd said to her on their counsellor's couch when she was talking about travelling and he hadn't understood. "It's not even real!"

Her eyes sting. The coffee sits, untouched, the cream a grainy slick on its surface. The sheets on the second bed are rumpled; Sarah has a dim memory of Ellie talking to her through the bathroom door, asking if she was okay, telling her she'd stay. Sarah covers her face with her hands, her fingers like bars.

"We've got fifteen minutes," Ellie says.

Sarah doesn't move, not right away. When Ellie's gone, she lifts the tiny nest of the note and pulls it open. *Do you still love me?* She does not know. She does not know what she wants. Why had she married him? It had seemed significant: the lure of his strong gravity, a place where she could settle, a place she wouldn't need to leave.

THE EARTH IS DRY at the Hohokam ruins. The true desert, before golf courses and resort spas. Sarah wonders how anyone survived there, but a sign posted along the dirt trail says they built irrigation canals. She takes notes, tries to focus on her work. Her hand tires, so she simply photographs the information on the placards.

When Lucas catches up to her, he looks awful: dark circles under his eyes, his pale skin pasty. The cuffs of his black jeans are cloudy with dust.

"Feeling okay?" he asks, and she grimaces. "Me, too," he says, then lifts the camera that hangs from his shoulder and takes her picture.

Together, they face the low opening of a red clay dwelling. Lucas stoops to go in and Sarah pauses, then follows. Inside, it is cool and dark. They are alone. He circles, holding the camera, searching for a good angle. For over a thousand years, the Hohokam lived in the area and then they disappeared. No one was certain why. She knows what Martin would say: drought leading to evacuation. Simple. He would be fascinated with this place. This is one experience she knows he would love.

"Happy family home," Lucas says, letting his camera hang.

"When's your flight," she asks.

He tells her.

"I don't want to go home," she says. Those nights filled with searing thoughts and worries, while, in the day, she'll spend hours and hours in the hard chair in her office, sending emails about stalled invoices, pitching query letters into echoing silence, then trying, trying, to write.

"Everyone has to go home," he says, and steps toward her, but his camera swings, hits her hard on the bone of her elbow. The pain surges fast and sharp and she sucks in her breath, curls her arm, stumbles back, stuttering an embarrassed apology like the one she delivered to him at breakfast the morning after the drunken night in Kentucky. Humiliated. Like it's her fault, only ever her fault, this vulnerability something to be ashamed of. Tears spring into her eyes and, suddenly claustrophobic, needing only escape, needing only to tend the pain, she turns to push through the narrow hole, into the hot, clear light of the day.

Dear Leila,
Dear Timothy

Nate wanted to do it at the beach. Tess wasn't sure, wasn't sure about much these days, but she followed along. It was the kind of thing her father would have called touchy-feely. She could picture him saying that, standing in his garage, cleaning wrenches with the oil-streaked rags that never got washed. If her dad was still alive, Nate probably wouldn't have suggested it at all, Tess thought, but then she bristled. Maybe she wasn't being fair.

It was November. Not the time of year to go to the beach. Nearly every day the sky spread over them like a cottony mass, shrouding the big lake before it dropped as cold rain, sometimes wet snow. Tess had heard the aggressive ring of the final bell at the elementary school up the street before Nate pulled into the driveway, surprising her. He'd left work early, he said.

Chose this day because she had called in sick, taken a mental health day. She knew what he was thinking: that she needed to do something, to take action, to get past it.

Get past it. All she could do was nod. She felt that if she opened her mouth, her voice might howl up into the white sky against which the trees stood now like charcoal marks. Ahead of them, the water lay flat, so stone-like its movement seemed thick, like lead pouring into a mould. As they stepped farther off the trail through the woods from their subdivision, Tess saw two kids, red and orange dots at the end of the beach. Their mother nearby, one arm lifted, a black dog pulling at the end of its leash, trying to get to the children. The dog's barking cracked through the air. Tess turned to Nate and spoke over the hushed sound of the water rolling onto the sand. "I don't want to do this with people here."

Nate shoved his hands into his jacket pockets and pushed forward, upper body bent, as if working his way through a gale. It reminded her of sex. All those times when she knew she was ovulating and, even though they were exhausted, Tess just home from her shift at the hospital and Nate wanting to watch the news, they went silently to the bedroom.

Sometimes she made him a shot of espresso first because she'd heard it sped up the sperm.

Him on top of her, toiling away.

They hadn't had sex in weeks.

"Where then?" Nate asked, tossing the words at her, as if he'd only just processed what she'd said.

She didn't answer. They were halfway down the beach already, had arrived on one side of a stream that trickled out of the forest and cut a path through the sand until it joined the lake. A naked log, smoothed by years, probably decades, of crashing around in the waves, beaten on shorelines and sucked under, stretched across the water like a bridge. The firepits were up ahead.

They could just have a fire, she thought. They didn't have to burn anything. Maybe even just go home and light it in their backyard, in the iron fire bowl they had received as a wedding present, registered for at Canadian Tire, but had used only once or twice. But she knew Nate wouldn't go for that. For weeks he'd been talking about this in that quiet way they had of raising the subject, letting it out inside the silence of the car, letting it prickle the air for a moment before they changed the subject: groceries, bills to pay, Christmas plans—like an ordinary couple.

Tess stepped onto the end of the driftwood. "Be careful," Nate said, as his hands lifted, hovered around her, like the extra-cautious person he'd been when she was pregnant, opening doors for her, helping her into the emergency room, onto the white cot, when she was barely ten weeks along. She'd done the positive test at three weeks and, as soon as they knew, he'd changed. He had started becoming a father, a good dad. Cleaned out the basement storage room, replaced the rotten stair on the back deck, seeded the bare patch of front-yard earth with clover. That was three years ago. Five failed procedures since then, acupuncture, herbs, thousands amassed on their credit cards, the house remortgaged, a stagnant adoption search…

Tess let out a breath, stretched her arms out to keep her balance. The bleached wood was slippery under her hikers, so she had to go slow. Two crows landed on the sand on the other side, and she heard the rustle of their feathers as they tucked in their wings. The people came closer, their dog off-leash now, the children running, the mother screaming commands—Sammy, come, Sammy, come, Sammy, come—even as the dog barrelled into the froth of a wave. The woman's arms lifted, opened to the air as if she were trying to gather all the chaos that had come loose from her, reattach the children, the dog.

But it was hers, Tess thought: that living fervour, those kids, sandy and damp and red-faced. To bring home for hot chocolate, to plunk into a bath. Her stomach clenched.

The crows shuffled toward the ragged aspen at the edge of the forest as Tess stepped off the log. Nate came up behind her as she watched the children, looping and spiralling, playing. Her eyes stung, but she could say it was the wind. He slipped his arm around her, and she felt the pressure of his grip through her puffy down jacket. They stood and watched the kids taunting the surf, running backwards from its hem of froth until one fell—the smaller, six maybe, maybe four—and a wave swept in and soaked her bottom, her legs. She started to wail, and Tess felt a pull in her, but Nate's arm lay like a root on her back, grown into her. The mother plunged in and seized the child by her elbow, pulling her to standing. She turned to the other: "You couldn't help her? You couldn't help your little sister?"

The dog, oblivious, bounded out of the water and charged over to Tess and Nate, its tongue hanging out of its face, spittle foaming against white teeth, so happy-looking he made Tess smile even as he jumped up and smeared her white jacket with mud.

"Sammy, down," the woman shouted, jogging toward them with one arm around the soaked child, hustling her along.

Tess wiped at her jacket, knocking off the heaviest streaks of sand. "It's okay," she said, before the woman could apologize.

The woman lifted one hand and tried to reorder all the fly-away strands of her hair. She gathered it, tucked it into her collar, and started to say something about the dog, a large black Lab, but the girl pulled on her arm. "Mommy," she said, and pointed at the boy. He was behind Tess and Nate, balancing on the log. He'd run around them, splashed through the shallow stream, to get to the driftwood bridge.

"Get off of there," the woman shouted, moving forward.

Nate grabbed Tess's hand and pulled her away from the family's storm. Calmly, they continued down the beach, the dog following for a short distance before he stopped and watched them go, ignoring his name, called over and over again by the woman until it lost all meaning.

"Maybe we should get a dog," Tess said, and Nate laughed.

"One like that?"

"Sure. One like that."

"But better trained," Nate said, and Tess shrugged. It was like him—wanting order—but Tess felt an attraction to the gangly beast, how it did whatever it wanted, followed its bliss, as her sister used to say when she was a hippie, before she settled down. Married a chiropractor, had four kids, was always complaining about her lack of time and freedom. The life Tess was supposed to have, everyone said, surprised at their divergences.

They stopped at the second firepit.

"Here?" Nate asked, and Tess nodded automatically.

She didn't speak, her voice a string that would draw out the tears like that doll she'd had as a child. The plastic ring in her fingers, the drawn chord, its mechanical voice—*Mommy, I'm hungry*—and then you could feed it from its plastic bottle, the contents magically disappearing. Didn't it wet itself, as well? Hadn't she changed its diapers? She tried to remember as Nate stepped into the nearby fringe of forest to rummage around, pick up sticks. She sat on the bench of a picnic table that had been pulled up beside the firepit. One end charred black, burned by rowdy teenagers drunkenly tipping the thing into the flames. Tess pressed a palm against her trembling lips. Inside her was this boiling, an unruly froth, like the sand and water the dog had kicked through, and she kept trying to put a lid on it, dampen down its hissing violence. The murmur of the family carried down the beach to her—the mother's voice turned to a shrill screaming, the now-cowed, silent children. Tess watched them disappear into the forest, onto the trail back to their neighbourhood. The dog the last to follow, running to catch up with them, to be put back on his lead.

When Nate returned, arms full of fuel for the fire, she was crying—silently—staring out at the horizon's sharp edge. If she let them, the sobs would turn her into a furious barking animal.

But she wouldn't let them. For so many years she had been hard, and the hardness helped. What would she be without it? Nate said nothing, but she could tell by the tilt of his lips that he was pleased. This was what he wanted, what the minister had suggested to him: "You need to grieve."

"Grieve," she'd repeated, when he told her, after his weekly counselling session, the appointments she refused to attend, not wanting to hear the same words her mother had used to try to soothe her. *It isn't God's will.*

"Grieve," he'd said again, as if the word was a name they were trying out, like the others they'd chosen in bed on weekend mornings, testing the sounds in their mouths. *Leila. Timothy.* What she didn't tell him was that she was tired of grieving, that she grieved all the fucking time: every month, every cycle, the constant disappointment punctuated by brutal streaks of blood on her underwear. Her body's persistent ignorance, its cruel refusal. And then the miscarriage, how it took her down and held her inside that wreckage, the walls caved in so all she could do was remain there, pinned under the dusty heaps, on the couch for days. She binged documentaries about terrible things—9/11 and Sandy Hook and serial killers—and streamed violent TV series about real-life murder. Nothing that had to do with her own normal life or how she'd once imagined normal life. Marriage, family, falling in love, their safe, secure neighbourhood.

Nate was standing beside her, she realized. His jacket already smelled of smoke. The fire burning. An arm around her shoulder. The wool scratchy on her bare neck. The flames flickered orange and yellow, blue-green at their roots. With his free hand he pulled a piece of paper out of his pocket. When he shook it open, she saw the blur of black ink and her stomach dropped. He'd done it. Written the letter. She'd tried but it was like writing to a dead person, a person who'd been gone for hundreds of years. An ancestor she'd never get to meet, so what was even the point of imagining who they were, what they looked like, what they had wanted out of life?

Nate's voice creaked slightly as he started to read. "Dear Leila, Dear Timothy." He paused and cleared his throat, then went on. His tone strengthened as he spoke over the sounds of the gulls and the lake. He read one page and turned it over and she stood and when he looked up at her, mouth still moving, she ignored him. She bent over, picked up a handful of earth, and threw it so it made pellets in the wind, spattered onto the sand, where it was smoothed by the waves. Nate continued reading— talking now about how he would have played ball with him, taken her to dance lessons, taught them both to drive. Things they'd spoken about over and over and over again. Fantasies.

The fire burned. Tess turned away. Nate hesitated, then kept on as she cast a glance back to signal that she was still listening. She kneeled on the cold beach and began scooping up sand in her gloved hands, building. Nate had written so many pages. He went on and on, and eventually she tuned him out, turned her attention to the crying of the gulls, the distant bleat of a train. Her hands worked, and after a little while she found she was surrounded by several fetuses curled in the damp sand. Flakes of dark bark for the eyes that opened at twenty-six weeks, a stage she had learned about but would never reach, her body simply unwilling or unable to make these things—these eyes or the tiny hands or the strong, beating hearts.

When Nate's voice finally faded away, they were both still, aware of what was coming next. The fire was nearly out, and he stood and tossed the last of the stick pile into the flames. When he walked off, she thought he was going to gather more wood, and she started to get up, but then she heard the rush of his urine and saw him standing there, turned away from her, one hand clasped around a young birch. From the tilt of his head, she could tell he was very close to crying. She realized she also had to pee, her bladder was painfully full, but she didn't want to move, not yet.

Circled by embryos, the ones she'd built, she waited for him to come back.

"Hand me a stick," she asked, when he dumped an armload of branches beside the shrinking fire.

He picked one up, a long one, and looked at her. "Do you want to say something?"

She shook her head, then stood, took the stick from him, and scratched at the dirt, breaking apart the shallow hillocks, pushing at their forms so the damp sand cracked and fell open. In a movie, they would have walked away, left the fetuses so the forms would gestate, be born by morning, then come and find them. It would be hilarious: a story about how suddenly their lives changed, from a grieving couple to parents of three fantastical children born out of a beach. How on earth would they explain that? As it was, Tess threw aside the stick and started flattening the swells with her feet. She stomped the soft earth with her hiking boots, grunting at the exertion. Pounding, slamming, kicking, breaking open those fictional fetal curls. Nate watched; he didn't try to stop her. When she finished, the whole area was smooth, like a lid of polished mahogany. Her heart slammed in her chest. She pulled in a stream of cool air, stuffed her fists in her pockets. And only then did he speak.

"Why are you doing that?"

She laughed, a quiet giggle, then curled a gloved hand over her lips.

"You didn't even bother with your own letters," he whispered. "You could listen to mine."

He held the pages tightly, fingers clenched, and she realized it was all he could see. Those lies: the perfect future they had each imagined and now had to part with, put away, erase with flame. But she had been living with it all along. Hope. Every month it had rolled in with the wetness of her body's tide, only to be pulled back out, hauling her with it, knocking her around. She was injured from the violent pitch and roll, tired of being submerged in cold fear in the night when she realized she wouldn't get the life she had imagined and, right now, she fiercely had to pee. She darted away from Nate, circled a fat elm tree, and squatted to empty her clenched bladder. The pee came in a hot rush, and she felt her insides soften. She groaned, relaxed into the crouch, felt the pull in her thighs, then wiped herself with an ancient tissue pulled out of her jacket pocket and poked it into the earth to decompose over winter. Back at the fire, Nate had his head bent over the letter, rereading, like a college student examining his essay's final draft. Above his head, a deep red soaked through the clouds, the first clear sunset in days.

Tess saw the tears on his face, and it hurt her to suddenly realize she didn't know if they would last. He straightened when he saw her returning and she tried to smile and so did he. But he was studying her, too, looking for something, a forward movement, the next step. She pinched one corner of the letter and tugged. At first he resisted; it tightened between them like a bedsheet. But then he relaxed, and together they bent forward to set the letter on the hungry flame.

WHEN THEY LEFT, night had come. They'd kicked sand over the fire until nothing shone through. Neither of them had a flashlight, so they moved slowly along the beach, soaking their feet when they crossed the narrow river. The trail through the woods was dark but well-worn, easy to follow because they'd walked it a hundred times. Out at the road, they met the woman again, walking her dog, alone now. The children at home, clean and in bed, Tess imagined, her partner reading to them or watching television, the dinner dishes piled to get to later, sand scattered over the bathroom floor. Or maybe everything in its place, immaculate, a predictable order established. It was impossible to say.

Tess held her hand out to the dog's nose, let him sniff her, then scratched behind his ear. He tried to jump on her again, but the woman pulled him down and made him sit, out of Tess's reach.

"You were there all that time?" the woman asked.

Nate nodded. Tess knew they were a mess—her hair tousled, jacket dirty, Nate's eyes swollen and pink from crying. She felt embarrassed, as if they were teenagers, caught having sex. The woman smiled at them, almost pitying, it seemed, but Tess didn't really know what she was thinking, if she was judging them or if she was jealous. If she was remembering when she'd been young, like them, when there wasn't anything that could hold her back. She felt a sudden warm pulse in her chest.

"Good night," she said, and caught Nate's muscular arm. His head jumped up. He looked at her, surprised, as she hauled on him, tugging him toward their home.

River's Edge

own by the river, where deer prints were pushed into soft mud, beside the imprinted treads of running shoes. Shiny white fishing line in tangled, tiny nests that fit in the palm of your hand, hooks with the barbs crushed flat, a lavender T-shirt torn and snagged in the dogwood's blood-red branches. That's where it happened.

I didn't want to go, but Marcie made me, hauled me by the hand through the shambles of the mid-autumn woods, sticks cracking. Skinny branches whipping back in my face. I felt the rise of criss-crossed welts on my cheeks, pressed my fingers against the bone of my jaw.

And still, she stomped forward, dragging me through the last weave of poplars to the shoreline, where the sky came clear. My ballet flats slapped into the muck, sent it splattering up my bare shins. I breathed out, bent forward. Marcie released me, moved away, squatted on a lattice of driftwood logs that were pale and skinned of bark.

I could tell she was trying not to cry. Her face held stiff, only her bottom lip moving, trembling like the wing of an early-morning moth. I studied her: blond hair scraggly, clotted in places, as if gum had gotten stuck in the strands, and even from a few feet away, I could smell her, that strong, sickly odour of baby power patted into her armpits every day after gym.

My shoes, real leather, dyed pink, and bought in Winnipeg for my birthday in the spring, were ruined. I tried not to care. Pulling free of the sticky grey mud, I stepped away from the river's frothy lip, closer to her. By then, she was sitting cross-legged on the mat of branches laid out over wet earth, so I joined her, gathered a lock of her hair, ran my fingers through to loosen it, to untangle the clotted weave.

For most girls this would have triggered tears, a stuttered confession, but for Marcie it was like I'd put a bandage on a wound, started applying pressure. With the point of one knuckle, she dug at each eye. I felt how her shoulders hardened, saw her face freeze deeper, as if it only mattered that we had arrived, reached the end of the race we'd gone on to get to that place, walking fast from school, through the construction zone where the road was torn open, a rusty pipe sticking out of the dirt, past the recycling trailers, into the forest behind the cement company with those rosy-cheeked people in parkas painted on the main vat.

Marcie had been showing the boys her underwear. I knew that. I knew they probably wanted more, were maybe getting more. A couple weeks earlier she'd taken me to the Dairy Queen in the uptown mall, bought me fries and an Oreo Blizzard, laughed with her salmon-pink lips, the colour blurring into a haze outside the lines. She pressed a crumpled twenty onto the counter, and I didn't ask where it'd come from.

A raven flew over, wings beating, calling out an electronic-sounding chortle like it had something important it was trying to say. I looked up, my fingers moving automatically, tugging, separating, a steady craft like beading, or my grandma's crochet. Marcie's gaze stayed on the water. Her eyes hardly blinking as she stared. I searched my mind and finally said, "It's low for the fall," repeating the words my dad had spoken that morning, on our way into town, after I missed the bus. "They must be playing with the dam upriver, over at Tobin," he said, but I wasn't sure what he meant. If the men in charge just followed their own whims, spun the wide metal wheel to let the water gush through or shut it tight, deepened the reservoir, let their buddies go fishing in a hundred feet, casting hard toward the flooded shore.

I know I should have asked her why we were there, what had happened, let her explain it to me in her own way, but I was afraid. Marcie's life seemed scary. Her arms were covered in fine scars from the razor blades she liked to run over her skin, and she told me casual stories about how her father beat up her mom, how she got lost in the woods once and was nearly adopted by a pack of wolves. Now her mother lived on her own in Swan River, three hours south. Marcie had moved in with her aunt and uncle in a ramshackle house near the dog kennel where the hard water had turned the bowl of the sink nearly entirely orange, where I didn't like to go because her uncle would always pretend he was Santa and ask me to sit on his lap.

A few times she'd run off, hitchhiked to Swan, and her mother, who'd lost a baby, who was trying to keep her job at Giant Tiger and finish high school, had to put her on the bus with borrowed money to send her back up north.

I went with her once, carrying a backpack full of chocolate bars, two cans of Dr. Pepper crushing the big bag of ketchup chips we ate while we waited for rides just a few miles out of town. None came to drive us south, and soon enough my father's headlights jumped along the gravel edge of the road. I knew by his face how much trouble I was in. Back home, stuck in my room because I was grounded for a month, I tried to suck off the bright synthetic red that had stained my fingertips, but for a whole day it wouldn't budge.

By the river, I noticed blood on the ground. My hands slowed to a pause in Marcie's hair. Her eyes had shifted from the current's silver ropes to fasten on the stain. Smeared into the mud, it could have come from anything: a gutted fish, the carcass of a muskrat washed up on shore, waiting to be picked clean by the birds. I felt a sickening drop in my stomach like the summer before on our family vacation, when I'd stood on the see-through floor at the CN Tower, stared down. I should have asked her what had happened. Instead, I said the next best thing. "You okay?"

"I guess I'll live," she said, looking down at her fingers. Their red nicks, black scabs. She picked at a line of dirt under a broken nail. Blue polish flaked off and she pushed at it with her thumb, sent it scattering to the ground where it shone like tangled fishing line.

My chest felt tight. Dampness seeped through the thin wool of my skirt. I swallowed, lifted a wing of her hair, started a new braid. "You sure?" I whispered, my heart beating in my throat.

Her head bobbed forward, a quick nod like a magpie before it leaps into air, opens its cloak of iridescence. Relief, I felt then, that I wouldn't have to know, that I could leave her unspent tears where they were, hidden like the river where it unravels into estuary, feeding secret wetlands, all those mossy bogs.

THAT WAS a Tuesday.

The next morning, a car from the local detachment was parked outside the school, flinging its red and blue lights against the damp brick wall. Rumours in the hallway like the slow leak of leftover helium. By noon, everyone knew about the knife, the one in her backpack, the one she'd carried south with us that day we'd set out unsuccessfully to hitch the two-and-a-half-hour drive to see her mother, while I brought the bag of food.

There was a boy with a punctured kidney, an older boy, sixteen, but he never came to school. That's what I heard, and that he was in the hospital and, eventually, that he didn't make it. A while after that, someone said Marcie was in Thompson, where a painting of a giant wolf watches over the town, where I live now, with my kid. All the time I wonder if she's still here, if I might see her one day. I imagine it: how I'll be picking through the withered grapes to find the salvageable ones at the grocery store, dropping green bananas that cost over a dollar a pound into my cart, and I'll look up and there she'll be, staring at me, waiting for whatever words I have to offer. What words do I have?

My parents still live in the same house, the one where I'd stand at the end of the driveway to catch the school bus, snug in my mail-order parka, and look at the water across the road. That year, after Marcie left, the river did what it's always done. Froze to months of white silence, then opened again in the spring. Ice plates carrying the winter's wreckage: broken-down sleds, abandoned fishing huts, whole trees with their roots torn from the river's edge. They drifted with the current before being pulled clear out of my sight. I watched them disappear; I went on with my life.

BUT THEN it happened.

Outside the high school, on a January morning that the radio announcer called both the coldest in half a century and the most depressing day of the year.

The line of vehicles was nearly lost in the mist of billowing exhaust, and kids ran from them like soldiers escaping enemy fire. My boy—Alfred, after my dad, even though it isn't a name I particularly like—caught up with his best friends and they jostled. Arm punches, headlocks, hip checks. The kind of casual physical intimacy that well-adjusted teenage boys indulge in. I felt happy seeing him like that. An affectionate warmth grew inside me as my gaze followed him to the school entrance, and there she was, standing off to the side, smoking, the tiny orange ember a beacon lifting to her face.

It felt like no time at all had passed.

It can't be, I thought, as I drove away, already late for work. But why not?

That evening, I asked Alfie if there were any new teachers at the school. He shook his head as his fork fished through the tuna-and-egg-noodle casserole I'd made. Eventually, I turned it into a game, encouraging him to list off every teacher who worked there, to tell me about their annoying habits. How Mrs. Carrier made them put their heads down on their desks in the dark if any one of them was acting immature; how Mr. Odubi called them all "buddy," acted too much like a dad; how Mrs. Slater made them put their phones into a plastic bin, even the visiting writer who'd come in that day, he said, describing how she had grimaced and then refused to part with her cell. The whole class held their breath because nobody said no to Mrs. Slater. I smiled. Mrs. Slaughter, the kids called her, and I pictured her scowling, gesturing dismissively, wiping her palms together like there was dirt on them, the dust of another era.

"Very well," she'd probably said. "Then I'll leave you to them."

Like the kids in the class were predatory animals, already circling.

I was living inside Alfie's story, my own imagining, so it took me a moment to realize that this was a new person he'd mentioned, this writer.

"Mrs. Linklater," he told me, "but she said we can call her Marcie."

My fork clattered against the edge of my plate; he didn't notice.

"She's pretty cool," he said, his eyes lifting shyly. I nodded, but I was no longer listening, and soon he drifted off, carrying his dishes to the kitchen. I followed. Scraped my leftovers into the dog's bowl, washed the crusty casserole dish, filled the dishwasher, hands moving automatically as my heart pattered. I thought about Marcie, about how close we'd been. How after she left—disappeared, really, it was that sudden—I felt the stinging agony that I had somehow failed her. The punctures in my secure, safe life had never really healed. They should have: father a foreman at the mill, mother the manager of the Royal Bank, all of us able to move easily through the world. Then I stumbled into Alfie's father. But that's another story.

The internet told me what I wanted to know.

Two books of poetry and a collection of short stories.

The short stories had won a big prize I'd never heard of, even though I like to read.

The web page for Alfie's school told me Marcie was there for a week, and tonight, at the library, she was giving a reading. I looked at the time. It started in fifteen minutes. Snow swirled against the window, rising from the deeper black. I hate going out at night, but I stood up. Walked into my bedroom. Changed into my favourite blue leggings, long black sweater, the kind of outfit Marcie might have worn back then, although her tights would have been crushed velvet, wine-coloured, paired with army boots, soles grey with caked mud.

AT THE LIBRARY, twenty or thirty people were crowded into the small event room. A child, five or six, sat cross-legged on the carpeted floor between the legs of a woman in the front row who was resting her hands on the dome of the little girl's head. Marcie sat beside them, turned away so all I could see was the gleam of her hair. Threaded with gold like the last time I saw her, on the river's edge, but from fluorescents this time instead of the sun. I sat in the second to last row.

The librarian gave the land acknowledgement, then read Marcie's biography. "Growing up in poverty," I heard. "Juvenile detention." Then, the words *poetry saved her life*. We applauded, and Marcie stepped up to the podium to face us, the audience, me just one person within this population, and I felt the greed inside me. I wanted to pop up and be seen, but when her blue eyes met mine for the slightest instant, they slid away with no recognition, as her fingers hunted through the pages of the book.

Applause rippled, and snickers of laughter, as well, as she read. A poem called "Virtue Signal" and an excerpt from a short story about an exhausted woman working late when an alien spaceship lands outside the strip club. Did I like it? Her descriptions painted beautiful scenes; I felt myself caught up in the story. I suddenly remembered a game we used to play, seated in the cold concrete basement room crowded with mouldy boxes where Marcie had made a fort.

"Close your eyes," she'd command. And when I did: "Where are you?"

I'd start to answer, but she would interrupt.

"Not here. Anywhere else."

She usually answered with cities: New York, Paris, and, one time, Marrakesh, a place I could not even imagine. How long had we been friends? The spring of Grade 9 through to that soggy autumn of Grade 10. We met when a teacher put us together to do a project on prisms, how ordinary light can be dispersed into its component wavelengths. I found it boring; Marcie did most of the work. Less than half a year we knew each other. I shrank back into my chair, shut my eyes, and listened. Her words slid by like ice sheets, bright and hard. When the reading ended, I stood in line to buy her books, gripped with indecision, unsure what I might say.

"I can sign them," Marcie said, after I slid my credit card through the white plastic square attached to her cellphone. "What's your name?"

My cheeks tingled, flushed pink—I could feel it.

"Julie," I said, and waited. Her pen scratched over the pages. Words filled my mouth like hunger saliva but where would I start? What could I say? Behind me, the lineup stretched all the way to the podium. Finally, she handed back the books and I leaned close, as close as I could, as if I were trying to sniff her out, detect that faint aroma of baby powder, but what I got was a clove smell, maybe citrus, a fragrance that brought no memories for me of the past.

"Congratulations," I whispered. It was all I could think of.

Marcie nodded, then blinked. She studied my face, glimpsing those memories maybe, like spotting something unfamiliar sliding by on the breaking ice. To me, it felt like we were locked again in that moment, down there on the riverbank, where something had happened with that boy, where she'd defended herself and suffered for it, and where I had resisted the only question that should have been asked: What happened? I could have let my ballerina flats fully flood with cold water, wilfully submerge into my own discomfort, for her sake. But I hadn't, and now she looked so different: hair twisted into a fat braid, makeup perfectly applied, successful, living a meaningful life while I had just spent my monthly entertainment budget and a bit more on her books. I wanted to tell her all of this, or something close to it. I wanted to ask her out for coffee, to catch up, to start being friends again, to laugh about how she'd taught me to dance in that foul basement, but I was frozen.

"Well, enjoy," she said awkwardly, as I stood there.

The person behind me muscled forward to take her turn.

Sitting in the car, I felt the weight of the books in my lap. The one on top, the short stories, was called *Hole in the Sky*, its title stark white against a wide, dark river. The water shone, holding the reflection of the stars within its muscular current. It was an image I had never seen, but why would I have? Safe at night in my childhood pink-and-green bedroom, dreaming about the future that would so easily unfold for me, or so I believed.

I wondered what Marcie had thought about her future back then. We'd never spoken about it. But then, there were a lot of things we hadn't discussed.

The car felt cold. The windows were fogged with condensation just beginning to sparkle into frost. I started the engine, blasted the heater, set the stack of books on the passenger seat. My shift didn't start until noon the next day, so I could stay up late. I would stop on the way home and buy a bag of chips with the change in the cup holder. Make a cup of sweet black tea, start a fire in the wood stove, and read. It was the only place I could think to go: alone, on the island of night, the world standing totally still.

Home Wrecker

The wooden siding is the colour of ash. Rot blackens the edge of the porch and all the windows are broken. Jagged points of glass glint, reflecting the light off the lake. Mark stops the car at the end of a laneway, two tire tracks worn into sand. He stares at the slick black shingles on the roof, the chimney spotted with holes.

"This is it?" he asks. "Your place?"

"Not just mine," says Jewel.

Beyond Mark's face, the lake is smooth as sheet metal, its surface welded by the sun. A storm is coming. It hangs in the air.

"Ours," she says. Mark raises his eyebrows. "The family's. We could go duck hunting." Jewel points to the forest. Past the pines, a marsh, her father's camouflaged blind, its remnants still there, wooden slabs and two-by-fours collapsed into a new pattern and shape.

"I don't hunt, Jewel."

"No," she says, pushing the passenger door open, swinging her legs out of the car. "I guess you don't."

LISA LOOKS THROUGH the window at her front yard, at the brown, burnt grass. Headless tulip stems and white Shasta daisies droop in the heat. Behind her, Ella sleeps in her crib, the sound of her breathing rising and falling beside the low, certain hum of the air conditioner. A red car passes on the street. Lisa watches the couple in the front seat, the man's hands on the steering wheel, his mouth moving, his head turning to the pretty blonde beside him and back again to the road. They are smiling. The phone is in Lisa's hand. She lifts it to her ear, presses the call button, listens to the empty dial tone bleeding into nowhere.

"DO YOU WANT to see something?" Jewel had asked that afternoon, her body turned toward Mark, away from the blur of dark forest at the edge of the road. They were driving aimlessly, bouncing down concession lines, searching out real estate signs while Mark advised her on what she should be looking for. High and dry, he kept saying.

Jewel picked at the bandage on her finger.

"Sure," he said, eyes straight ahead, focused on the ruts in the road.

"It's a place."

He glanced at her, wary. "What kind of place?"

"You'll see," she said, pointing to the gap in the trees that would take them there.

Inside the house, their feet grind into glass and the floor's debris. Mark follows her, pressing his footprints over her smaller ones before he leaves her trail and steps into the kitchen. The counter is cluttered with grimy glass jars, rusty lids, a knife with a blackened blade. Jewel watches as his eyes sweep through the room, examining, absorbing, his gaze sliding from the unravelling braided rug to the cellar door, which hangs from one hinge. Outside, billowing grey clouds swell in the sky. Her skin, wet with sweat, waits for relief. A piano sits against the back wall of the parlour, its polished top cracked from moisture, a few keys pried off. In the corner, a china cabinet, the wooden shelves occupied by three empty bottles, beer and rye. It was half-full of china plates and teacups when Jewel's father first brought her here on her ninth birthday, after they'd gone hunting. Six mallards lay in the back of the truck, the green of their bellies gleaming. He'd invited Lisa, but she wouldn't come. "I won't kill anything," she'd said, chin angled up, arms crossed, like a statue. She stayed behind, but at the house their father picked out a single cup to bring home for her, hairline cracks threaded through several perfect rose petals.

"But it's my birthday," Jewel had complained, standing beside the cook stove, the chips in the white enamel turning orange with rust.

"Sweetheart, this whole place is yours," said her father. The cup hung from his hand by its handle, half hidden behind his leg. "All yours. Only yours and mine," he said.

Jewel knew it was all pretend, what Lisa called his stories. She looked around, wondering at the secrets of the house.

Her father sat at the crooked kitchen table, setting the cup where a cup should be. "Will dinner be long?" he asked, feigning annoyance.

Jewel stared back at him as he rested his hands on the table, fingers intertwined, waiting. Awkwardly, she turned her body to the stove. "Almost ready," she said, and she did what her dead mother had taught her: opened the oven door, looked inside at an imaginary chicken, skin crackling, no longer bloody at the bone.

"It's so hot," Jewel whispers now. The words everyone has been saying for days, complaints of the heat muttered between condolences. Stating the obvious, her father would have called it. Mark looks up from the counter, a spent shotgun shell cupped in his hand. He doesn't say anything. She wonders what he's looking for, if it's the same thing she has tried to find, burrowing into the decay, seeking the family's remains. Forgotten money. Bones of a baby they couldn't afford. He turns to the wall calendar. *October 1936*. That imaginary time she and her father spent here, him sitting in a lawn chair in the living room, out of work, reading the newspaper, while she scratched dinner out of cracked jars filled with pretend peaches and the winter's last potatoes. Cutting out the black spots.

"Dad brought that here," she says. "He found it at a yard sale. He said it just fit."

"Brought what?"

"The calendar."

Mark nods as he moves to the empty window. "When was it built?"

Jewel shrugs. Her armpits prickle. The afternoon darkens as if the light has dropped out of the day. She remembers the rain. Beating on the thin tin roof. Erasing every other sound. She adjusts the skinny straps of her tank top, gone slack on her bare shoulders.

Mark's eyes are fastened to the lake. Like a sailor. Staring out to sea. Looking for a place to land. She takes a step forward. His eyes shift to her face. "Great resale value," he says.

She doesn't know if he's joking. She smells him, the spice of sweat and musky deodorant, and moves closer.

"Jewel," he says, and then his cellphone rings, the noise blasting from his pocket at the exact same time that thunder rumbles in the distance. He pulls out his phone, and Jewel begins to count to figure out how close the storm has come. What she wants is to reach out, grab the sky, tuck it under all the corners of the house, patch the glass, re-brick the chimney, repair the stairs, steady the floor so they can move easily, extend themselves in comfort. Tucked into a pleat in time. Folded inside someone else's memories. Hidden.

AT HIS HOUSE, a couple days ago, the sharp edges of a bottle cap bit into the bottom of Mark's foot. "Shit," he snapped, bending over for the stray cap and two others that had slid under the table. The empties were lined up by the breadbox. He grabbed a Canadian for himself and walked to the sliding glass door in the dining area, then back to the fridge for another beer. Jewel lay on the lounge chair on the lawn, her eyes hidden behind white-framed sunglasses. Another bottle stood beside her, stuck in the yellowed grass.

"Ready for more?" Mark asked. When she lifted her head from her magazine, he saw the muscles in her stomach tighten. Her bikini was blue, spotted with coppery-black dots that gleamed like oil. He held up the beer.

"Sure," she said.

He walked toward her, gesturing at the baby monitor on the picnic table. "Still asleep?" he asked, rolling the volume dial, relieved to hear the deep in and out of Ella's breathing. He glanced at his watch. "She actually shouldn't sleep this late," he said. "Lisa…"

"Lisa," said Jewel, tipping the last dribble of the old beer into her mouth. She opened her legs, only a crack, only to uncross her ankles. He handed her the new bottle, and she pressed the cold glass against a mole on her chest. Mark took a drink. He shoved a hand in the pocket of his shorts, then turned away, nose prickling at the strong scent of her coconut sunscreen and looked at the fence he'd built last summer. The apple tree they planted when they found out Lisa was pregnant, after the second in vitro. Most of the leaves were brown and withered. Mark walked over and fingered the remaining green growth. He pulled off the dead leaves and they crumbled in his hands. Through the monitor, Ella cooed. Mark turned around, stared at the small white box, the grid of the speaker.

Jewel sighed. "You know what I've been thinking?"

"What?" Mark asked, sitting on a lawn chair.

"I've been thinking about taking my five grand and buying a chunk of land."

"Yeah?" said Mark. Dark bits of leaf were stuck to his fingers. He wiped them on his shorts.

"Build a little house. Have a garden. Bird feeders. A cat."

"What kind of house?"

She looked at him, rested her chin on the bottle's lip. "I don't know."

"Frame, brick. You could do something cool like straw bale or—"

Inside, the phone rang. Ella wailed, the sound blasting through the monitor.

"Fuck," said Mark, standing. When he slid open the door, the air-conditioning chilled him; he shivered as he picked up the phone.

"WAS THAT LISA?" Jewel asks, as Mark slides his cell into his pocket. He nods. "Nothing important," he says, fingering the table's edge like he lives there. Jewel knows he doesn't want to tell her, doesn't want to break the moment, bring Lisa through the door. She's already here, Jewel could tell him, but she doesn't. She leaves her sister in the corner, in the shadows, arms crossed, watching.

LISA PUTS the phone down. Softly. As softly as she can. She steps over to the counter, which is cluttered with bouquets of lilies and red roses and pours herself a cup of cold tea left over from the morning. She puts it in the microwave, pressing Stop two seconds before the timer goes off. Milk. Sugar. A seat at the table. On the other side of the centrepiece that Lisa made herself out of dried flowers from her wedding is the wooden box holding her father's ashes. She stares at it, sipping her tea. Too sweet, she thinks, imagining opening the box. Pouring the ashes, bits of bone and skin, singed slivers of fingernails and calcium deposits and kidney stones, and the black gristle of his congested arteries, into a measuring cup. A quarter cup, a half cup. Baked into a cake, then sent to her sister. She would watch as Jewel ate it, enjoyed it, licked the icing off her fingers and asked for more. Then Lisa would tell her. She would watch her sister choke on their father's body. Sick. She takes another sip. Definitely too sweet, she thinks, as the baby begins to cry, as thunder rumbles in the outside world, as the afternoon shrivels away. She gets up, pours the tea down the drain, places the cup in the sink, wipes crumbs off the counter with the edge of her hand, and dumps them into the compost bin on the counter before walking the long hallway to the nursery at its end.

"SHE'S CRAZY," Lisa said that morning, picking wadded tissues off the floor by her side of the bed. She threw them in the trash, then rifled through a tray of jewellery on the dresser. Tugging at loops of gold chains, plucking an amethyst earring out of the mess. Mark left the room. Lisa followed, sliding the post through the hole in her earlobe as she walked.

"How she was with my dad," said Lisa.

In the kitchen, he opened the fridge and closed it again, turning to face her. "Do you blame her? You can't pretend that—"

Lisa snorted, her top lip jumping up in an ugly snarl. He stepped back, startled. When he looked at her again, she was normal. Her face composed, small clumps of mascara caught in her eyelashes. "What did she have to complain about?" she said, her voice shrill.

Mark stared at her. When Lisa's gaze shifted away, he said, "At least she's looking after Ella. She's trying to help."

"Yeah," said Lisa. "That fills me with confidence."

Mark shut the cupboard door so hard it cracked through the quiet room. Their heads turned together to the baby monitor. Ella smacked her lips, a sound that once would have made them meet eyes, delighted.

"She wouldn't even see him," said Lisa. "He asked for her and she didn't even come."

"We could get a nanny," Mark said.

"No, we can't," Lisa said. "Not on one salary."

"What do you want me to do?"

"You always want to do something. As if you can fix everything." She left the room.

Mark opened the cupboard door again. "Crazy," he said out loud, staring at the gleaming metal cans with their bright labels, looking for something to eat.

When Lisa came back, she found him sitting at the table, a salmon sandwich in his hands.

"Did you want one?" he asked. She shook her head. She rubbed the bottom edge of her lipstick with one finger and smeared the red onto her chin, but he didn't tell her. He took another bite as she told him about Ella's extra bottles, the brand of wipes that irritated her skin, things he knew and she'd already written out for Jewel.

She stood in the doorway, watching him. "My shift's done at ten," she said. His mouth was stuffed with salmon and celery and gummy bread. He chewed quickly, trying to swallow. She sighed. "See you tonight then," she said, and left before he could speak.

AFTER THE FUNERAL, people stood on the back deck at Mark and Lisa's house, eating macaroni salad and cold cuts from paper plates. The local radio station played Phil Collins and WHAM!, and her dad's friends from the assembly plant sat in a clump of lawn chairs, pulling Labatt 50s out of the cooler, drinking silently and smoking, dropping ashes on the lawn. Lisa eyed them, unsure where they were headed, if they would stay late into the evening, lurching around her house, fighting and breaking things.

In the bathroom, Jewel refreshed her lipstick with some of Lisa's, fixed her hair with Lisa's brush, applied purple eye shadow and Lisa's black mascara. When she was done, she went outside and leaned against the railing. She put pieces of cheese and meat into her mouth and swallowed red wine.

"Are you okay?" Mark asked, appearing beside her. Jewel shrugged. Sweat showed through his thin white shirt. His purple tie hung loose around his neck.

She wanted to reach out and tighten the knot, slide it closer to his throat. She couldn't answer his question. If Lisa had asked, it would have been different. Lisa wouldn't have waited for an answer. She would take control, grab Jewel's hand, squeeze it firmly, coldly, then drop it loose into the thick, hot air.

We're fine, she'd say. *We're fine.*

Mark watched her.

"I'm fine," she said, resting the glass between her breasts. "How are you?"

"Mark," Lisa called, stepping through the door. "Ella needs changing." The square heels of her shoes pounded on the wooden planks as she approached.

Jewel turned and Lisa saw how she'd made herself up. Lips dark red. Purple bands on her eyelids like she'd been punched. How her body leaned toward Mark, her breasts white against the low, scooped neck of her black dress. Lisa hadn't even seen her cry yet, not when she had appeared at Jewel's apartment with the news or even when they stood together at the crematorium. Earlier that afternoon, in the church, tears ran down Lisa's cheeks and she'd felt Jewel staring at her as if judging.

Lisa reached out and wiped the pad of her thumb against her sister's rouged cheek. "What's on your face?" she asked. Jewel stumbled backward, wine spilling onto her dress.

"Lisa," Mark said.

"Don't," Jewel said, pushing Lisa away. She plucked the light fabric of her dress away from her wet skin; a red rivulet of wine trickled between her breasts, and Mark watched. Lisa saw him. Even as their cousin stepped forward with a napkin and Mark moved back, he was still watching Jewel mop at her chest. The crowd stared at them.

"The baby," Lisa snapped at Mark. When he was gone, she leaned in close to Jewel. "Making Daddy proud?"

"You're fucking psychotic," Jewel said.

"I think you should leave," said Lisa.

Jewel laughed. "You're kicking me out of my father's funeral," she said. "For the record." She picked up the glass and downed the last inch of wine before pushing past Lisa, close enough that Lisa smelled her scent. The musky odour of the perfume Mark had given her for their last anniversary.

THAT NIGHT, Jewel drove to the house. She nearly rammed her car into a grove of aspens, then stumbled inside the wreckage of the kitchen, her tears mixing with the grime on the table to make an oily black mess. Beyond the smashed windows and the rotten planks of the front step, the lake churned violently in the moonlight. When she finally stood up, it wasn't to leave. Instead, she lit a candle. In her high heels, she walked to the counter and pretended to cook. Her father in his lawn chair in the parlour, reading while she made dinner. She sang "Chattanooga Choo-Choo," and when the food was ready, she set the table. She wrapped her fingers around the cracked back of the wooden chair and said, "Come and get it," and laughed, out loud.

LIGHTNING STABS the sky. Wind thrashes the long limbs of the white pines, dropping dried needles onto the car. Mark stares out the window, lips pinched, brow furrowed. He clutches his phone. She knows her role. She's the one who brought him here, encouraging him up the narrow dirt road, through the overgrown forest, telling him to keep going, to ignore the red *No Trespassing* sign pocked with bullet holes.

"Do you want to go upstairs?" she asks. She has never been, was always stopped at the bottom by her father, laying his large hand on her shoulder, saying it wasn't safe. She's always dreamed about the upstairs—its perfect bedrooms with floral wallpaper and iron bed frames and white curtains snapping in the breeze. She walks across the room. Her foot on the bottom stair.

"It doesn't look…." Mark begins, but she doesn't stop. She climbs and the rain starts, roaring in her ears like it used to. Back then. Back when she and her father sought shelter, sipping sweet coffee from his steel thermos, both of them someone else, somewhere different. Lisa, back home, betraying the truth.

"TO BUY LAND?" Lisa asked.

"I thought he could help me look."

They were on the phone. Jewel's hands busy with a knife.

"Ella. No, sweetie. Not yet."

Jewel waited.

"Oh, for Christ's sake," Lisa hissed, her hands wrestling with the squirming baby, the diaper only half on. "Hold on," she said. She put the phone down and finished the job, ignoring the bile stinging her throat. "What are you going to do with land?" she asked.

"Build a house."

"You should move to the city. Start fresh. Don't get stuck here like me."

"I'm not."

"Right," said Lisa. "Twenty-eight years old, still working at—"

"I'm fucking not."

"Not what? Twenty-eight or still working?"

Jewel didn't speak.

"Oh, right," said Lisa. "Your choices are your choices."

Jewel stared at the apple in her right hand, the knife in her left. Two ham sandwiches and a pile of sliced carrot sticks sat beside the cutting board, ready to put into lunch bags. She rested the blade against her fingertip. Delicately, she sliced. "I have to go," she said. "I cut myself."

Lisa looked toward Mark, who was digging his hiking boots out of the closet. "Well, back by five o'clock, okay?" she said. "I finally have a day off, and he promised dinner out. We've got a sitter."

After she hung up the phone, Jewel pressed a paper towel against the wound. The sting felt clean. Like polished silver. Sunlight caught in still water. The silence when all is past and over, without any regret.

AT THE TOP of the stairs, Jewel pulls her foot free from a hole in the rotten wood and grits her teeth against the pain. Blood sprouts from her bare shin.

"Are you okay?" Mark calls, his voice raised over the storm. He grips the banister with one hand. A bolt of lightning brightens the house. He stares up at her. "Come down, Jewel."

"Are you afraid?" she asks, and shimmies back to the window, a hole looking out over waist-high grass, the remnants of an old garden, dead rose bushes, brown lilac blooms.

"This is crazy," he says, but he sets his foot on the bottom stair.

Two steps from the top, Mark goes through. Face opening in a sudden ugly exclamation, he lunges at the landing. She grabs at his arms and chest, and he digs his fingertips into her skin as he pulls his leg out of the jagged wood and climbs the last stairs. Safe, he sprawls beside her, his breath coming ragged and fast.

"We really should fix that, honey," he says, and they laugh, holding stiffly to each other on the sagging floorboards.

Water drops in shiny rivulets from the mouldy ceiling. Three closed doors lead into three different rooms, rooms that Lisa and their father had explored. The one and only time Lisa came. Jewel outside on the porch, arms crossed, watching through the once-intact window as Lisa moved through the house, marking the dust on the floor. At the bottom of the stairs, she stood and stared up, and before their father could say anything, she'd climbed to the top.

"It's just a stupid old house," Lisa called down from the landing.

Jewel watched her father. She waited for him to tell her to come down, to get out, to get going, to go on home. She was wrecking it all! Instead, he put his hand on the banister, his face tilted up, and Jewel saw that he had forgotten her, that she had ceased to exist. Upstairs, he and Lisa disappeared. Nothing but a rumble of voices crossing over her head, then silence, then the rain.

"Are you all right?" Mark asks, pointing at the scrape on her leg, the blood rising in fat, shiny beads. It stings. Her body hurts. The heat has already broken and she feels very cold, the sweat on her skin turned to an icy skim. His hand hovers near the wound, lingering there, then touching. Hot on her chilled thigh.

"Don't," she mutters, but when he pulls away, she reaches out. His gold ring is a hard stone caught in her fingertips, like one she could skip if the surface was calm enough. His breath catches, a gasp beneath the deluge of the downpour, then a groan. She pulls him toward her, doubling their weight on the floorboards as thunder quakes the shell of the house.

Extraordinary Things

Corinne was married once. When she lived in Seattle. When she cut her hair so short, scars showed up on her scalp like pencil shavings. One afternoon her husband came home drenched in salmon-coloured paint and told her he'd been laid off from his job at the renovation company. She was seven months pregnant. Outside of Eugene, Oregon, up a hill by some hot springs, she had the baby. Danny was tripping on mushrooms when her water broke, and one girl went to find him while another spread newspapers on the floor of a broken-down school bus. Something went wrong. She drifted into darkness. Woke to a black silk dress, a hat that her mother made her wear. A coffin so small and shiny it looked like a wooden box for holding photographs. Danny in the doorway. Face ashen. Hand tight around Corinne's shoulder. Holding on.

OUR HOTEL ROOM looks down on an overgrown park where teenagers meet for dates, kiss awkwardly at dusk. In the distance, the volcano steams. William's monkey sits on the dresser, chewing wands of sugar cane, its red leash trailing down to the dirty tiles. It turns nuts over in its tiny hands and drops papaya seeds onto the floor, the sound like far-off firecrackers, like that all-night dance party we went to a month ago in Argentina. "You have to be careful with it," Corinne tells me, as if I'm concerned about the monkey at all, as if we have a relationship. At that party, she and some Czech guy got together. When she woke, the sun was glowing through the grape leaves and her jeans were soaked with mud. As she climbed into the top bunk at the hostel, I was shaken awake. "Hey," I whispered, but she didn't answer. Just rotated toward the cement-block wall and stayed like that until morning wore away.

Corinne and William met the third night we were in town. She and I were switching hotels because we kept coming back after midnight and the owner would tell us off as he unlocked the door. William was watching TV in the lobby of our new place, and I recognized him as he laughed along with the other men when Corinne confused the word *key* for *ham*. He had these dark eyes, this black hair. He didn't notice me. I was standing behind Corinne but I could still see her blush, the colour spreading across the back of her neck.

A RED SCARF on the doorknob is our signal. Already I've been to the hot baths three times, hiked into the foothills with a Russian girl, gone down to the river with two teenagers from Brazil, dragging my fingers through the soft ash as they talked in Portuguese. I've asked Corinne to come with me, but she doesn't. She buys fruit at the market. Flies crowd around the green and red rinds in our garbage can. She goes to William's family home for meals. The first time, his mother touched her sixteen times. She counted.

WE HAVE BEEN here a week and I am ready to go to the coast, but Corinne won't leave. She stays in the hotel room or sits in the park reading an English novel she found in a bookstore in Quito. Her skin is pale. The monkey climbs around the room as if looking for a way out. I don't like when it walks on my bed, but she doesn't do anything. It is like that here: all these abandoned creatures poking their noses against you, prodding your hands open for food. Stray dogs, even an orphan, a little boy who lives off scraps, bits of chicken and rice given by local families and the occasional dinner bought by tourists he's learned how to charm. By now we are known in this town. It is almost empty. Most people left when the volcano erupted three weeks ago and only some have come back to protect their property from looters. Banners and signs mark the evacuation route, and the ancient frescoes in the basilica show scenes of dark orange lava flowing beneath angels floating barefoot in the sky. Sunlight stings my eyes when I leave the dark church. I go to a French restaurant recommended by my guidebook and eat fish with stewed tomatoes and look at my watch, waiting for evening to start.

I don't mind being alone. But not in foreign places where I don't know the language. It's like I'm carrying a small glass bowl and often I drop it and catch it right before it shatters. Like a superhero. Saving the day. Scooping it out of the air moments before it hits the pavement. But rather than victorious, I feel shaky. Like even though it didn't break, there's a crack, and something's leaking out.

MOST OF THE COBBLESTONE roads in this town end at dirt paths that snake up into the mountains. There's an artist who hikes down and spreads his paintings on a llama-wool blanket for tourists to buy. Scenes on stretched-skin canvases of peasants in traditional hats and ponchos, some holding curved scythes. The sky on each is a different colour. Mustard yellow. Aqua blue. A menacing red-pink above the flat-topped volcano. The paint is a hard lacquer, like nail polish. I've purchased two of them. One to remember the place by, the other for Corinne.

WILLIAM IS AROUND all the time now. Corinne looks after his pet monkey like it's also hers, as if they share custody. Soft and grey, it sits in her arms like a slip of something else. A shadow of the baby girl she bore and lost. That much is obvious. Everyone knows that. Even Corinne's mother, who has become friends with mine and ends up with the phone in her hand when I call home. I tell them things they want to hear—humongous papayas, groundhogs grilling on spits in the street, all the beautiful waterfalls.

"A monkey," Ellie says. CBC in the background. Coffee mugs cracking on the new granite countertop. "Well, maybe that's good for her."

"She likes it enough," I reply.

"As long as she doesn't try to bring it home."

"Of course not," I say. William and the volcano go unmentioned.

AT NIGHT, I DREAM about Thomas. The last time I saw him was in the fall in Toronto, at the end of an ice storm. Fishtailing down a side street while I cried in the passenger's seat of his car. It was all too complicated, he said. Too wearing.

Like I was a hard thing. Rough and abrasive. Rubbing away his skin.

On the airplane back to Vancouver, I flew from dusk into bright day and my nose kept pinching like I was breathing fumes from a solvent. I visualized him getting smaller and smaller, swirling down the drain. After midnight, my mother picked me up at the airport and I announced that I thought I'd be travelling soon. Bigger places, I meant. Not Canada.

In one of my dreams we're at a restaurant. Thomas at the head of the table, holding the hand of another woman. Birds are stuffed in a bronze-and-black coffee thermos and the patrons eat them by biting off their heads. The waitress ignores me. There's also something about the volcano. A flood of lava. Disintegrating glass. But I can't quite remember that part.

TONIGHT IS the opening of William's uncle's bar. When I get back from the restaurant, Corinne is putting on makeup. Her black eyes widen in the mirror as she coats her lashes with dark brown mascara and turns her face side to side, gazing at her sharp cheekbones, appreciating the weight she's lost when her hippie husband used to tell her she was too fat. We never talk about that, about the weeks after the coffin went into the ground beside her 102-year-old grandmother and all she did was eat and sleep, numbed out on Ativan, sopping up her leaking milk. I watch her as, down below, the kids gather to couple up and walk a few circles around town before ending up back at the park. Corinne takes a cigarette out of my pack and shakes it. The filters rattle but we've never cut them open to see what's inside. I light one and toss the pack of matches onto her bed.

"William," she says, as the small fire flares, "asked me to marry him."

An explosion of smoke when I laugh. I wave a hand in front of my face, push the window open, and sit on the sill. The street band is playing. They play every day. Usually I don't hear them anymore.

"He did," she says.

"I don't doubt it," I reply.

We stare at each other. Ants crawl over the sticky floor. Our room smells like rotten mango and decaying earth. The mushroom smell of sex; something slowly rooting.

"I'm sure you'll be very happy," I say.

"You don't have to be like that."

"Like what?"

"Like a stupid, privileged white girl. Like you can't see anything past your stupid pink nose."

I stare at her as she forces one shoe off with her toes and then the other and sits cross-legged on the bed. Loose threads loop like miniature mountain ranges and she plucks at them, pulling them out. Finally, she lights her cigarette with a snap of a match, then taps the ashes onto the floor.

"Don't do that," I say.

"What? They clean. They'll clean tonight."

"Only if we ask them."

"Don't you think we should?"

I look at her. As if I am the messy one. As if it is me devouring fruit, shedding hair, dropping my dirty underwear all over the place.

CORINNE WAS FRIENDS with my sister in high school. After she and Danny broke up and she moved back to Vancouver, she started coming to the Y where I worked. She came for Tuesday afternoon boot camp. I knew what had happened to her but I didn't say anything, just filled her in on my sister in theatre school in Toronto and tried to ignore how impressed she was, how overeffusive.

"Getting rid of the baby fat," she said one day. Her eyes touched mine.

"That fucking sucked," I said.

After my shift we went out for beer. We talked about all the places we wanted to see. Three drinks in, we started planning our trip.

AT THE BAR, the monkey sits on the counter. William's cousin strokes its head. William's uncles sit on straight-back chairs, drinking. They dip clay mugs into a collective bowl and pull out a cloudy mixture that tastes sweet and sour. Corinne shuffles a deck of cards. The hem of a woman's blue dress sways, and the orphan boy stands in the doorway, smoking while he watches. William leans back in his chair, tapping a rhythm on Corinne's shoulder. His eyes float around the room until they land on me. There are bodies between us, breaking our gaze. We take a drink at the same time. A skinny teenager who pointed out the word *blonde* to me one day in the dictionary asks me to dance. The uncles fill my mug again and again, and the alcohol dulls the fact that I am waiting. Before we were here, we were in Quito, Ecuador, where a pickpocket tore open the side pocket of my cargo pants and stole fifty American dollars without my even noticing. Three weeks ago we were in Tilcara, Argentina, where there were not enough hotel rooms and we had to share with a college boy headed for Bolivia. He kissed Corinne on a large flat rock by a cemetery full of plastic flowers. Bright fuchsia against the gravel-covered graves.

Corinne doesn't know it, but I met William first.

I touched him first. He touched me.

When we were still in our first hotel, I went out to buy tampons one evening and the street band was playing. As I walked by, his damp hand seized mine and I laughed as he pulled me against his body. His palm felt hot against my lower back. Sweat prickled my armpits as I turned in circles, uncertain of the steps. "Tranquilo," he breathed in my ear. Back with Corinne, I held on to the sensation of his voice in my ear like a secret, something that was only mine.

In our new room, Corinne was sorting through her under-wear and dirty T-shirts, separating them into piles. "Your face is all red," she said.

I started to tell her but then stopped to light a cigarette. She held a pink-and-silver thong in one hand. With the other, she reached for a drag. Smoke leaked through her lips when she asked me what I thought of the dark-haired guy from the lobby whose name we didn't yet know, who I'd already danced with once. I opened the window to let in some cool air. "He's cute," I said, and that was all.

CORINNE RESTS her fingers on the table's edge, squats beside me. "Cramps," she says.

"Should I go with you?"

She shakes her head. Stands up.

One of the uncles refills my cup.

"That stuff is deadly," she says, but her eyes are clear, much clearer than mine.

I'm already seeing the fringe of a fuzzy second layer from the alcohol, so I leave the cup where it sits as the uncle speaks to her in Spanish and she answers but no one translates. When she reaches the other side of the bar, the monkey climbs into her arms, and William leaves with her, winking at me before they step through the doorway, into the dark.

After they've gone, I take a slow sip and light a cigarette. Leave it burning in the ashtray and use the point of a pen to dig open the filter of another. Inside are black nuggets of charcoal.

I make a pile on the table. Fuel for a cold English cottage. The uncles laugh. My blackened fingers beckon one of them to dance. We circle the floor. My body caught in his confident motion. His wife watches, hands clapping to the rhythm of the rondin and guitar. Over the man's broad shoulder, I see William return. He watches me. When the song is over, I join him at a table in the corner. All the women's eyes are sharp as pins. Even the uncles are staring. But my thighs open to his hand under the tablecloth and I am swimming, held by the wet heat of wanting more. Hovering over danger. Asking it to suck me in.

Outside, William pushes me against a wall, leans his groin into mine. I resist, slightly, laughing as I lightly slap him away. "Isn't this why you're here?" he says in sudden, crisp English, right into my ear. "To get a lay?"

And then Corinne is back. White like steam in the dark street before her face comes clear. She stares as I shove at his arms and laugh. Pretend we've only been playing, and say, the words warm stones in my mouth, "He was just walking me home."

HUNGOVER, VOMITING in the bathroom down the hall and hoping I don't clog the toilet. Corinne stays with me. Like a mother, she leads me back to the bed, dampens a washcloth, and lays it on my forehead, asking again if anything happened. "I don't care," she says. "I just want to know."

"We were playing," I tell her.

"Pretty serious playing."

"You have a brother," I say. "It was brotherly."

"The dancing gets pretty hot," she says.

"Uh-huh."

"So it got hot?"

I lift a flap of the blue cloth and squint at her. "Are you going to marry him?" I ask.

"I don't know."

She lights a cigarette. I point to the window. She stands up and pushes it open. The strange songs of foreign birds float up from the park.

"I know it's only dancing," says Corinne, turning back to me. Over her shoulder, ash floats down from the sky.

Corinne goes out to buy bananas, bread, and coffee. She leaves a bucket beside my bed. The sour green liquid gushes out of me with no warning. Tenderly, I touch the small bruises on my thighs. They throb hotly like some sort of monitor.

THOMAS CALLS ME into the living room. Nudges the air with the remote control. "Isn't that where you were?" he asks, as I turn up the heat. The middle of a hard January and I am always cold.

Cobblestone streets. The sharp staccato sound of the flute. The television camera enters the church, illuminates the worn frescoes of past eruptions. Thomas starts to talk, but I hold up one hand. Lava runs down the dirt trails, and I think about William, his family, the artist from up in the hills. Corinne came home pregnant. The baby is eighteen months. Last I heard, they were waiting for William to arrive.

That morning after the uncles' party, I decided to go to the coast. To leave Corinne and William behind and take a boat to the Galapagos Islands. Wear a see-through rain poncho. Point my camera at yellow-skinned iguanas, sloppy sand nests of tortoise eggs, enormous birds that are clumsy on land so they soar in the sky for weeks. All sorts of extraordinary things.

Tenderloin

Carol had never seen anyone so dirty. The man's fingers looked ink-stained from filth, and scabs covered his knuckles, seeping, oily. The sutured skin of an amputated leg poked out from the ragged hem of cut-off blue jeans. When she saw him, sitting in his wheelchair at the corner of Geary and Leavenworth, she didn't even notice the woman standing behind him until she spoke.

"I'm Monica," the woman said, extending a slender hand to Carol's husband, Ed. A gold band gleamed against her skin. She wore her hair in a large afro, high and round, a hallmark of another time, the seventies, and Carol had to resist staring.

"This is Garfield," Monica said, and the man in the chair lifted two fingers to his temple in a salute, then smiled, showing a bright set of teeth. "It's not so bad as it looks," he said, gaze skating from Ed to Carol, and Carol felt her cheeks burn. Easily,

Monica gripped one of the wheelchair handles, as Ed shoved his hands into his pockets, a sure sign he was nervous.

"Thank you for meeting us here," he said. "Where do we begin?"

"You brought a picture?"

"I emailed one—" Carol started.

"We did," said Ed, cutting her off.

Carol looked at him. She had sent an image, high resolution, of the twins in their penultimate year of high school, one of the last they'd taken of Chloe. The girls looked happy, Chloe beaming at the camera, Lena's head tipped back in laughter. Matching plastic bibs around their necks. The evening they'd gone for lobster to celebrate Ed's fifty-eighth birthday. She'd thought about cutting Lena out of it, using Photoshop, but what did it matter? They looked almost exactly the same. If you were looking for one, you were looking for the other, to a stranger's eye.

Ed flicked his fingers toward Carol, a gesture she knew meant *hurry up*. Anger bolted through her. He was irritable, but she was, too. Her heart sat in her throat like a tight ball of tinfoil, ricocheting off her fillings whenever a car horn sounded or a streetcar screamed against the iron rails. She had not yet adjusted to the time change, and the clothes they'd brought— shorts and T-shirts—weren't warm enough for the cool afternoon's threat of rain. And it was his fault they were late. At the motel, he had received a call from the mill while they were unpacking. Something about a breakdown in one of the dryers, and as his voice had climbed to that reedy, demanding pitch Carol hated, she had stepped quietly outside, sat on a plastic patio chair near their door, and closed her eyes. The smell of damp ashes rose from a tulip-patterned teacup on the ground that held a dozen cigarette butts, orange filters imprinted with lipstick marks, veiny, bright pink. Did Chloe smoke? No one in her family had smoked. Now, waiting for what would happen next, Carol fingered the black plastic folder in her hands.

"I already sent one," she said, as she pulled out another copy. Monica reached for it, then looked down at Chloe's face.

"Don't trust the email," Garfield said. "And definitely don't download any apps. All they want to do is follow you, everywhere you go." His grey eyes flickered up and down the street, hunting the shadowy corners. And that's a bad thing? Carol thought. At least then she'd know where her daughter was, but she stayed silent, trying not to meet the suspicion of his gaze, to not think of his mother, his family, the people panicked with worry about him. Or maybe he had no one. Maybe he was utterly, totally alone. Monica nodded her head.

"Yes," she said, and sighed, and suddenly they were in a different reality, one in which Chloe was alive and known, a physical being instead of the flickering image of a little girl drowning in a slushy, stagnant pond in Carol's terrible nightmares or an adolescent pressed into two dimensions in her aging school photograph on the dining room wall.

dear mom, the email had said. *i thinnk am ready to go home im n the tenderloin*

Carol's hand was shaking so much she struggled to click open the message with its *[no subject]* subject line, could hardly focus to read the words. When she did, she quickly realized how much more she wanted. Exact coordinates, not this slight whisper from far beneath the wreckage.

Her breath came out in a long exhalation as if she'd been holding it in for seven years, two months, and eight days, and she pushed her trembling fingers, knuckles creased with white flour, against her lips. When she lifted her eyes from the computer screen, the room looked suddenly shabby and old, the cracked arms of the overstuffed leather chair by the fireplace, the towel on its seat covered in a mat of grey cat hair. The mess of her books. The stack of newspapers and magazines opened to recipes waiting to be clipped out, experimented with, improved upon, until she made them her own. Cheating.

She had a deadline for a draft of her new cookbook—*Savory Cookies and Cakes*—that she wasn't going to meet. Everything tasted like chalk or caustic, as if laced with chemicals.

She stood then, stumbled over to the window, and yanked open the curtain, remembering the roar of Chloe's boyfriend's refurbished muscle car seething through the open windows, the kind of car Carol herself had driven around in the 1970s, smoking pot, once even snorting a line of cocaine through a rolled-up Canadian ten-dollar bill. That abrasive engine's thrust had hauled her out of bed night after night to find her daughter's room empty, the window open, screen plucked out of its frame. The hammock of stuffed animals hanging from the ceiling, the Teletubbies poster still taped to the back of her door covered up with photographs of Chloe's friends and her boyfriend, Ivan, beach parties and east-coast sunsets, like a collage of a perfect daughter's carefree life. It was all still there; they had simply shut the door, left the room as it was for the past seven years.

"Drugs, Mom," Lena had said to her once, four, possibly five, years earlier. When she was still in university. In Carol's mind, this idea hadn't been so bad because that meant there would be a road back, a path to take to return. Rehab maybe. A nice place by the ocean. In the seventies, she had heard so many stories about friends and friends of friends who got lost for a while then became stockbrokers, even lawyers. Yuppies.

"What?" Carol asked. "LSD? Marijuana?" And, even though the word was a new one for her, still loaded with a meaning other than the chemical: "Ecstasy?"

Lena had laughed, her head swinging lazily, that mocking smile on her face she'd perfected in her late teens. "Try crystal meth, Oxycodone, bath salts."

Carol opened her mouth but nothing came out. Lena tapped her temple. "Those drugs burn out the dopamine receptors in your brain, so even if—"

"Stop," Carol said, and sank to the floor. One of those days, it had been. Under her, the plush beige carpet. New, Carol remembered, so it would have been six years ago, after they'd used her first advance to replace the old carpeting, laden with years of cat dander and vomit stains from Percy, the rescued chocolate Lab they had for four years until he succumbed to liver failure. Chloe had been inconsolable for weeks.

CAROL HADN'T BEEN able to reach Ed to tell him about the email. She called Lena but there was no answer. Lena was probably in class, lecturing about genetic constructs, DNA spirals, science she spoke excitedly about at family dinners, her cheeks flushed, white wine rocking in the stemless glass while Jake, her husband, cut their son Graham's chicken. Carol felt jealous of Jake's willingness to be an engaged father, to change diapers, boil organic yams and mush them up. When the twins were born, the parenting tasks had simply fallen to Carol. That's how it was in those days. Was that what had happened? A single moment of impatience, a split second when Carol pushed away Chloe's clutching, sticky hand when she should have wrapped it in her own, loving, mother's grip. At two in the morning, three, four-thirty, she wandered the dark house, wondering about that, the thought a slow, stubborn growth, building its rings. Had this splinter of rejection lodged itself in her daughter's heart, festered there, grown punky until its toxin started steering Chloe's life?

Was it her fault?

Of course it was her fault. She was the mother.

So why hadn't she seen it coming? That was the question she tortured herself with over and over again. Almost every day for the past seven years, going back in time, pressing her hand against her daughter's flushed, tear-swollen face, doing what she hadn't done. Pulling herself out of the wind tunnel of everyday life in which she made Black Forest ham sandwiches for paper-bag lunches, filled Ed's thermos with black coffee, paid bills over the old-fashioned kitchen phone, tried to learn the new computer, worked the day job she had then as an X-ray technician where she saw every day the obvious hard facts of bone and skeletal structure, the ghostly inner reality of other people's selves, while her own daughter gradually excluded her, hardened her exterior, and eventually faded away.

MONICA HELD THE PHOTO out for Garfield to see. "Her," he said with a growl. He pointed a finger at his temple and spun it in lazy circles like the kids used to do.

"What's that mean?" Carol's voice sounded shrill.

"You know her?" Ed asked, eyes wide.

For a moment, Carol wondered if he'd thought she'd made it all up—the email message, their lost daughter's plea. She looked at him. He pressed a hand against her shoulder blade, and she held her breath, thinking *wouldn't it be easier?* To spin back the clock, reverse-walk through the airport, let the plane suck up all the exhaust it had spewed out over the continent, and withdraw to their quiet house. Grandparents. Only a few years until retirement. Her successful second career doing the baking that she loved, that had kept her sane, if a bit heavier than she ideally wanted to be. Ed had bought a third-hand sloop he was slowly fixing up. They planned to move south, buy a cottage on the Gulf in Cedar Key, closer to Lena.

The irony. After years of wishing she could have done just that, gone back in time, into Chloe's childhood, like a detective, and kept a keener watch. On the soccer coach or the son of their neighbour across the street who'd moved back in with his mother in his forties, who played his guitar on the front step as he watched the twelve-year-old twins ride their bikes up and down, up and down, until fireflies studded the dusk. The grey bristle on his face, his gaze tethered to their slender limbs. All the terrible, unproven suspicions Carol continued to heft, that Lena assured her were baseless. But they weren't together all the time, were they? They couldn't have been. Twins, but so different. Each with her own set of friends, and Lena with so many more than Chloe ever had.

But no, not her fault. Of course not. She was here now. The hope in her felt ravenous, not like a thing with feathers but with fangs and claws and an insatiable, violent hunger. On the other side of this howling need, Monica was speaking. Ed nodded along, his mouth pinched, eyes sunken in that fearful look she'd seen many times: the day their first baby came out stillborn, when he faced his younger brother's liver cancer, when his aunt died by suicide, when he was laid off from his job, when Carol herself had broken down, ended up hospitalized for two weeks as they sorted out medications to help her, the plastic-looking capsules she now took daily.

Monica was saying something about how Chloe had used their services, then about addicts, about cycling drug use, ups and downs, the efforts to heal. "There's a crash period," she said. "That may have been when—"

"Take me," Carol said.

Monica looked at her calmly, assessing. Carol felt her heart beating, the shivering, fearful pulse in her throat. "Just…" she said, and then Ed's fingers groped at her shoulders, crawled around to pull her to him, to hold her. She fought not to cry. She stepped away, shrugged him off her, ignored the quick flare of pain in his face.

"Take us to her," she said.

Monica nodded. "I'm advising you to be prepared."

"Of course," Carol said, even though she didn't know how to do that. Prepared for what? She didn't know what Monica meant.

"SAN FRANCISCO, MOM," Lena had said when she finally called back. Carol did not tell her how she'd envisioned a slab of raw beef, glaring a wet red before purpling like an aged bruise. The expensive cut, one her mother would have rarely purchased at the downtown butcher shop with the creaking wood floor, the dusty cans of corn niblets and cherry pie filling. The butcher, Fred, with his brown-streaked apron, his relaxed way with blades and slicing machines. His own daughter had died at eight, Carol remembered her mother telling her once. Drowned. She'd felt astonished when she heard that, could not attach the image of a little girl floating face down among the bulrushes and lily pads and leeches to him, his easy nature, his glass jar of multicoloured jawbreakers sold for ten cents apiece, his pretty, red-headed wife who worked the cash but rarely spoke, smiled without showing her teeth.

In the background, Graham hollered, *Here, here, here*, and Carol heard the sound of his tumbling footsteps, then car doors opening and closing.

Finally, Lena spoke into a pocket of silence. "We're just leaving the dentist," she said, and Graham murmured something about Sylvia, the doll he couldn't go anywhere without.

Carol thought of her own girls at that age, spinning on the filthy orange shag carpet in the cramped motel room where they lived for a month after moving to Maine, where Carol had killed earwigs by the half dozen as they crawled out of the rotten window trim. Was that the kind of place where Chloe was now living? God help them, did she have a child?

"Hello?" Lena said. "Did I lose you?"

"I'm here," said Carol, and Lena told her about that part of the city, the Tenderloin. Drug addicts, prostitutes. Sex workers, she called them.

"Where are you getting this?" Carol asked. She didn't want to believe it. San Francisco, for her, was the city of love, a place she'd travelled to in November 1969, with her girlfriend Gail. When she talked about that trip, at parties, to new friends, she sometimes called it her last little bit of freedom and did not tell the truth: how Haight-Ashbury had been much grubbier than expected. Not at all soaked in a pure golden California light. She and Gail had hooked up with a house of hippies, crashed on their living room floor, tried magic mushroom tea, ate bowls of chewy brown rice and a salty-sweet lentil stew, and woke up starving and bleary-eyed in the middle of the night. When she returned home she'd met Ed, at a party in Port Arthur, where the power went out and they sat around drinking rum, telling ghost stories, wrapped in the host's grandmother's knitted afghans. He walked her home. They sipped milk warmed on the stove in her kitchen and tried not to talk too loudly, until her mother called to her from the dark hallway, admonishing, advising her to say good night to her guest.

At the back door he gently touched her wrist. Slowly they leaned their heads together until their lips met. Twelve months later, she was married.

"Google," said Lena. "Just google it. She's given you a neighbourhood. That's a pretty big clue, although…"

"Although what?"

"It will still be difficult. It's a rough place. You should find a guide."

"A guide?"

"A cop. No, maybe a social worker or somebody who works at one of the shelters. Somebody like that."

Her elder daughter, older by almost exactly three minutes, had always been the practical one, her head tipping toward the logical, the answer to the equation. Sometimes Carol felt angry at her for growing up so easily, transitioning into a reality where she hardly ever mentioned her own troubled twin, except occasionally, and with a kind of Republican cruelty. *She made her own bed*—that sort of thing. Chloe had been sensitive. Chloe had read poetry, even wrote it, until her Grade 8 teacher had returned a two-page poem about the changing of the seasons covered in red scrawls. *Awkward, overdone, the romantic's covered all this.* Carol circled the horrible teacher's grammar mistake with pencil, the pressed lead glittering, and gave it to Chloe to bring back, but Carol found it later, torn into shreds, the crumpled strips tangled with a desiccated black banana peel, at the bottom of her daughter's backpack.

"And be careful," said Lena. "Be guarded. Take money, not a lot, but enough to grease the wheels."

Carol nodded.

"Mom?"

"I got it."

"Let me know what happens. Call me when you're there."

Carol laughed, a quick, sharp guffaw that even to her ears sounded hysterical. "We haven't even booked the tickets yet," she said, wiping spittle off her bottom lip.

"But you will," said Lena. It wasn't a question or a command, simply a statement of fact.

Carol felt a rush of love. How well her daughter knew her. She nodded again, then said, "Of course, my darling," her words fading into the strain of a whisper, caught behind the gush of tears that always seemed ready but rarely came. Lena was holding on, and Carol knew it was up to her to say goodbye.

"Take care of my grandson," she said, and hung up, laid her forehead on the cold surface of her closed laptop, and sat up again almost instantly, started to plan.

"THAT'S TENDERLOIN," the cab driver had said when Ed told him the intersection where they were meeting the social worker. With his accent—Russian, Carol thought—the words sounded gauzy and thick, as if he had cotton batting stuffed in his cheeks. His eyes flickered over Carol's face in the rear-view mirror, and she stopped herself from picking at the gummy edge of a piece of duct tape covering up a tear in the vinyl seat.

"I know," said Ed. "Just, please, drive."

MONICA TOLD GARFIELD she would catch up with him later. "Vietnam?" Ed asked as they walked away. Carol cringed at the assured knowledge in his voice, like he was used to war vets, how damaged they could be. During that war, they had been in Canada watching it unfold on the hand-me-down black-and-white television set Carol's mother had given them. But Monica shook her head. "Iraq," she said. "Two tours. We're trying to get him a place."

Across the road, a crowd snaked along the wide sidewalk toward a saggy striped tent where people were giving out foam cups and bowls. A plastic bowl of dinner buns glowed on the portable table like an orange star. Carol watched Garfield wheel into a circle of men, then picked through the other faces.

"She won't be there," Monica said.

"How do you know?" asked Carol, but Monica didn't answer.

They followed her into a rooming house in an elaborate Queen Anne building with blistered purple trim and up a dark and narrow flight of stairs. Carol gripped Ed's hand and he pulled her; her knees cracked in the cold silence. From deep in the building, a woman groaned, and when they hit the landing, Carol smelled something sharp and chemical, like battery acid. She pulled a clotted tissue out of her pocket, pressed it against her nose.

THE ROOM WAS in a turret. The windows and outer wall curved. The door had cracked open when Monica knocked, and now she and Carol picked their way across the carpet, through discarded clothes and CDs, a laptop torn in two. Monica wrestled one of the windows open, letting in a bombardment of car horns, a woman shrieking *cocksucker*, as Carol stood in the centre of the room, feeling the thumping of her heart. Behind her, Ed stood in the doorway, watching Carol moved toward the bed, her hand reaching out to drift over the tiny roses on the coverlet.

"Be careful," Monica said, as Carol reached into a pile of books. Three or four of them set in a crooked stack, half hidden under the sheet. Sylvia Plath, Gwendolyn Brooks, other names she did not recognize. One had a garish cover, poppy red, and she lifted it up, clutched it against her chest as she turned to Ed. He seemed unable to look at her. Arms crossed sternly, he stood with his hands stuffed into his armpits, as if fighting off frostbite. His face had paled and fallen, despair dragging down his cheeks. Next to him, at waist level, she saw a mist of brown blood on the fading ivy-patterned wallpaper. Monica's phone let out a burst of crickets, and Carol watched as she looked at her screen.

"There are other places we can try," she said. "We can have lunch first. We can talk—"

"I'd like to wait here," said Carol.

"Carol," said Ed.

Carol crossed her arms around the book, steadying herself. Her eyes dropped to the filthy carpet, to a plate holding half a sandwich, the bread flushed green. A suitcase lay on the floor as well, hinged open like a dead clam. A pair of shiny black tights coiled around a single high-heeled shoe, the kind Chloe would never have worn, and a sheer yellow blouse with a ruffled collar that Carol picked up, leaving the book in its place. Small, so small, almost a child's size.

She held it to her face, the delicate fabric easily crushed in her palm. She caught her daughter's scent, the perfume Chloe had worn in high school, a mix of essential oils Ed's sister had made for her. The fragrance came to Carol like the delicate strand of a dream that slips away as soon as you try to hold it, follow it back to its source. She lowered herself to the bed, suddenly unable to stand, the ground an unstable edge, surrounding the hole of Chloe's disappearance.

"I'm so sorry," Monica said.

"For what?" Ed asked.

Monica did not answer. There were many things to be sorry for, Carol knew, her daughter one pale facet among so many. A single shard from several broken lives. But Carol's life was broken, too, she realized, in this room haunted by her daughter's absence. The sense of her, all around, yet impossible to touch and taste. A missing ingredient. The flattening effect of forgotten baking soda; the vacuous shadows spotting strangers' lungs on those X-rays she'd once captured, signalling threats.

"I can't leave," Carol said.

"Carol," Ed snapped.

She stabbed a glance at him as a hard thing pinged off the filthy window, but they ignored it, all three of them, breath held, as if needing the twine binding them in that strange, hushed triangle to snap. Then a penny flew through the gap in the opened window and bounced across the carpet like a flat stone. Monica spun around, wrestled the window open, and leaned out.

"I seen her," Garfield shouted up at them.

Carol leapt to her feet, the yellow blouse now twisted around her wrist like a cuff she held tightly looped as she bolted toward the door.

Only later, after they'd chased to exhaustion the shadow of their daughter, did Carol think of the window, left agape, open to the evening's pounding rain. She would have to clean it up.

Grass Fire

Arthur's lips had that twist to them that said he wanted to be left alone, but then he suggested we go for a walk. I'll admit it was a nice day. Late summer, butterflies flitting over the swamp milkweed in our native plant garden by the back shed. More monarchs that summer than I'd ever seen, although the internet said they were dying off at an alarming pace. My friend Sharon liked to post those stories on Facebook, but I found myself looking away. There's only so much a person can take, especially me, especially lately.

I had barely slept. This recurring dream about drowning kept coming back and coming back, and once it woke me that was it. Arthur didn't like me to leave our bed in the night, had been like that for thirty years, groaning in annoyance and laying a heavy palm on my wrist if I so much as flickered toward my side. Lately, though, he'd been more flexible. Letting me be, twisting away, his back turned to my insomnia, the occasional night sweat. Giving me some freedom, I thought, so I could sneak out, retreat to the guest bedroom, where I kept whatever novel I was reading or a crossword puzzle in progress.

That night was particularly bad. A car, plunging off a bridge into a mucky river. I couldn't escape. My hands hit and hit at the cold, hard glass; it was immovable, a rigid layer between me and my life. I woke, always, moments before the water's darkness took me, in a panic I gulped down so as not wake him, even though he no longer had to get up early to go to work.

For seven and a half months he'd been retired, although you wouldn't have known it by how often he went back. Several times a week—almost every day, if I'm honest. Clean-shaven, wearing cologne, as if he still had an office to get to, that heavy oak desk to sit behind that had been signed by every editor going back to 1922. Rumour had it the desk and mostly everything else in the old building—the darkroom trays and developing chemicals, the newer digital cameras, half the computers—were about to be auctioned off, but that wasn't our concern, was it? He'd had his career and now it was over and yet I still found myself slipping chicken salad sandwiches into brown paper bags and sending him off to do God knows what. I couldn't even ask.

I thought about phoning—talking to Colin, the city hall reporter, or Melinda, who oversaw the obituaries and classified ads and had a way about her I didn't wholly trust. How her voice cranked to an artificially high octave like she was always begging. Occasionally I picked up the handset to do it, to say, *Have you seen my husband? What is he doing there all day?*, but I suspected that the inquiry would get back to Arthur, and I didn't want to deal with that. His cold annoyance, his silence as we ate our last meal of the day across from each other at the dining room table, with CBC radio playing from the stereo on top of the credenza.

A walk. Late summer. The heat having eased.

It had been ages since we'd done anything apart from grocery shopping or medical appointments, those outings he long ago determined we should do together, on a regular schedule, even though that had also changed.

At my last physical I found myself alone in the waiting room for the first time in years. It was so strange that if I closed my eyes, sitting there, I could feel the pressure of his invisible form filling the seat next to mine, both of us waiting for my name to be called. When I was pregnant, we'd done so many of those appointments together that I think he established this idea that it was okay to keep coming in with me for every little problem. Bladder infections. Bad headaches. My frozen shoulder.

That's what I said to him, anyway—the doctor, not Arthur—when he expressed concern about this over the telephone. The next time we went in, he told Arthur I should see him on my own, that I was *a grown woman*, and Arthur didn't speak to me for days. Communicated solely with his silence, a sort of psychic bristle that irritated my skin but that I couldn't escape, like an allergen. Pollen or smoke from a distant forest fire filling the atmosphere when you've no choice but to breathe.

You might be wondering why I've stayed with him for so long.

Sure you are; I know I do sometimes. Often, in fact. Every moment when I try to do something he doesn't like and he treats me like an unruly animal, needing to be ushered back in line, his stern, silent face nudging at my heels. Nobody asks for a life like this, to be pinned down in such a way, but I married young, and in those early years it seemed like one tragedy after another heaped themselves on top of me until I ended up in the hospital. The narrow, creaking cot on the fourth floor holding me like I'd been tossed back up on a stony beach, mind flooded with the flotsam of a million currents.

I was in no fit state to move on, to try to resuscitate my fledgling teaching career, to support myself. I imagined myself in a kind of servitude, living out my years knitting toques and thrummed mittens, canning salsa from our fresh garden toma-toes, scattering food for the pretty blue and orange fish Arthur liked to collect in a large tank inset into the living room wall. Hoping—if I'm honest, if I'm truly honest, and if I can't be honest here, then where?—that he might end up like one of those men who isn't able to retire and drops dead their first Monday free from work.

This is a sad confession, I know, but, as my mother used to say, there are many ways to live a life, and this is the way I've lived mine: under a heft of cascaded rubble, sipping at any available air. Sweet it is, though, when it's so rare.

"A walk," I said. Still woozy from the dream, that dark gush pounding behind my eyes. Only halfway through my first cup of coffee.

"I'll get some things ready," said Arthur, surprising me. He went and pulled a water bottle out of the cupboard, filled it at the sink.

I felt edgy, unsure of how much time I had, so I carried my mug upstairs and drank as I dressed, sipping slowly so I would not choke.

WE DROVE WEST, into the flat spread of farm fields, the canola turning more green than buttery yellow, nearly ready for harvest. Arthur swung down a dirt road. He had packed a picnic in a basket a long-dead aunt of mine had given us for our wedding twenty-seven years ago. The wicker was disintegrating; it crackled when he lifted it, needing a ginger touch, but I bit my tongue as he heaved it roughly onto the back seat before we left our driveway. I'd seen him slip a bottle of wine inside, one of the reds left over from last Christmas that was much too heavy for the season, and wondered if he had some news, if there was something to celebrate. A vague prickle of excitement filled me as we drove, a sensation I hadn't felt in a long while. Maybe he'd planned a trip, the cruise up into Alaska I'd always wanted to take, or a week in the tropics once the weather turned cold.

When we parked at the nature preserve, I got out of the car with a fresh energy and trotted after him along a mowed trail leading into big bluestem, rudbeckia, goldenrod nearing its bloom. Bees flitted from flower to flower; I recognized mourning cloak butterflies and tortoiseshells and even a couple of monarchs.

He was silent as we walked. Halfway around the loop trail, the pathway petered out, so I waded after him through the tall wild grasses until I looked down and saw a scattering of ticks on his pale, bony ankle, hungrily starting their climb up his calf.

We ran the rest of the way. Laughing. Laughing and shrieking, yelping, fuelled by the invigoration of escape. At the large sign in the parking lot, I drew in gulps of air as we kicked off our shoes, plucked the roaming ticks from our shins, our knees, the fabric of our clothing. Finally I glanced up and down the empty road to make sure no one was coming and undid my shorts to drop them and look down, to pull out any that had hidden in that dark, while Arthur watched.

He waited until right then to tell me. As I stood outside in my underwear, ticks crawling through my unshaven leg hair, one already fastening, I could feel it. Tiny head burrowing, body ballooning with my blood as Arthur pulled me close and held me, his voice hot in my ear, breath sickening, an old man's breath I steeled myself against as usual, not wanting to reveal my disgust.

"I'm sorry," he said. "I didn't mean for this to happen. I've known her a long time."

I tried to escape. Flailed in the muscular grip of his arms, but he would not let me go. Roughly, he stroked the back of my head, muttering *shush now, shush*, until my only choice was to swallow my rage and succumb, elbows pinned against my abdomen. There I stood, half naked, captive in the shadow of the large sign that explained how prairies are made. How they need to be burned to the ground, blackened by fire, for any new shoots to grow.

Triple Feature

After my father died, my mother started developing cravings. It was as if she was pregnant, as if inside her she was growing a new life. Hot dogs heaped with sauerkraut, sliced strawberries layered with whipped cream. One day it was pumpkin pie, and when I couldn't find the dessert anywhere in town, I had to make it from scratch. I helped her as best I could, but all she was doing was eating, so mostly I just gathered food, fired the stove, sat back, and watched. She had no friends to help her; no one called except the coroner with the results of the autopsy, which my mother never talked about. In a way, it was as if my father were still around, gazing at us from his old army photograph on the wall beside the kitchen table while my mother grew fat on her grief. It wasn't until later, long after my father's funeral, that she started thinking she had a thyroid condition, and when she spoke about her illness in social places like the grocery store, people—women mostly, my teachers, the parents of my long-gone friends from high school—would nod compassionately while I lowered my eyes to the speckled tile floor because I knew the truth.

THE DOOR INTO the projection booth is open, and Frank's in there, looking at his cellphone, texting slowly with two prodding thumbs. When I enter, he blinks up at me in the dim, flickering light, then flips his phone closed, drops it into his pocket.

"Can you leave it?" I ask, meaning the projector, because normally he does. He gets the film going and runs downstairs to check on focus and alignment, then back up to make any corrections. After that, we work together in the concession, ladling the butter-and-oil mix onto popcorn, twirling cotton candy, before he has to kick out the rowdiest kids.

"It's been wobbling again," he says, pressing his foot against the heavy iron base to steady the spinning machine. It's nearly forty years old; when it goes, that'll be it for the old Palace Theatre, and then I'll be out of a job.

"What about tomorrow night?" I ask, because it's the unofficial start of summer, the season's first triple feature. He gives me an exaggerated shrug.

I nod and step over to the small, smudged port window. A minute ago the hero and his mistress were in his hotel room, the camera zooming close to their reflection in a martini glass as they made love beside the speared olives. It's now morning and their silver convertible curves along an oceanside highway, the woman's red scarf slipping loose to ride over the cliffs in the wind. In a few seconds, the credits will roll, and Jonathan, my boyfriend, will still be sitting there, popping one cold kernel after another into his mouth, as if expecting more.

I fell in with him by accident when he came him to the show. He'd just moved to town to teach Grade 10 English and replace the pregnant guidance counsellor. At the concession, he bought a bag of Klondike Gold gum and a large Coke, and when he reached for his wallet, I saw the flash of his silver flask, engraved with cursive script. "You gonna tell on me," he whispered, like we were fourteen, sneaking our parents' booze. He wore a black leather duster jacket like Keanu Reeves in *The Matrix*, jeans, and desert boots, and his eyes were a mischievous gleaming blue that seems to have since flattened to ordinary grey.

"Enjoy it?" Frank asks, easing his foot away as the audience streams toward the lobby. A few people disappear through exits on either side of the screen. Back in high school that was where we'd get high, lean into the rattling chain-link to look down at the dam's frothing water.

"I've seen it four times."

"Occupational hazard," he says. It's what he always says. In the morning, he'll ship the film on the Greyhound, toward its next stop along the Trans-Canada highway.

Frank's the same age as my mother and balding. His remaining hair is soft and dark blond, and he hardly has a belly under his denim shirt, sleeves rolled up to show off his forearms, tanned from fishing on Lake Matinenda. He looks like Almanzo from *Little House on the Prairie* or maybe a casual Giles from *Buffy the Vampire Slayer*, but with a narrower face, fuller lips. When he stands, he shakes out his leg, stomps one Doc Martens on the concrete floor. The machine begins to vibrate again and its stream of light shivers, blurs the letters on the screen.

"Anyway," I say. "Total rip-off of James Bond."

"You think?" he asks, and turns to flick a light switch beside a faded poster for E.T., edges curving inward and torn. In the sudden burst from the fluorescent tube, I smile, expectant, waiting to hear what he'll say next, but there's the muffled ding of an incoming text, and the phone is suddenly cupped in his hand.

"Have you built up the reels?" he asks, staring down.

"Who's that?"

"We need them done, Des."

"Marie?" I can't help myself. I want to know.

He doesn't answer, and I don't say what I'm thinking: that I'm not actually working, that Angie, his niece, is doing the snack bar, that I actually came on a date and I should go home, get some rest, because tomorrow night we'll both be up late.

"At least do the first film," he says, so I sigh and run back downstairs to give Jonathan my car keys, to tell him to go ahead to the bar, that I might be a while.

BY NOW, MY MOTHER is obese. Her calves are like water balloons covered in a fine, felt-tipped scribble of purple and red. I've spent much of the past decade swinging those heavy legs onto her bed before withdrawing from the prickle of hair she can't shave without help. Even now, with the home-care nurse who does a lot, who comes to our house while I'm running errands and working at the theatre, I feel the repulsion. It's a stiffening, an arming, a way of holding my breath while I plump her pillow or tap out pills, hold them to her mouth so she can gobble them off my palm like a dog. I've often wondered if this hardness, growing inside me, gathering layers like a gallstone, is the reason I'm stuck.

"*You're just like your father,*" she hisses whenever I raise the idea of abandoning her, of moving in with Jonathan. That shuts me up. There are words I'd like to scream, lob through the stuffy, thick distance between us, but I can't. I can't because I know she's a little bit right. Some days I want to do what he might have: walk into the nearby woods, keep going until the big lake, cross the water in a motorboat, figure out where I am once I get there, set up camp on that opposite shore. Or else jump on a railcar bound for the west, take the bus south to the city. Head out to find glory, to become some sort of hero. Sometimes he'd be gone for days, but he'd bring back gifts. Chunks of fool's gold, morels, once a baby turtle that we kept in an aquarium until I set it free in the neighbours' pond. Dark duck meat breaded and sizzling in the electric fryer, a moose hung by its ankles in the garage, blood draining. Would I do that, too? Come back hauling souvenirs? Animals I'd killed for food? No. If I ever manage to leave, I'll be gone for good, off into my perfect life, living it up.

THE REEL ROOM is dark, small, and stifling. The first time I saw it I thought of the wardrobe in those kids' books, furs pressing into your face before the back panels open to Narnia. I pull the light bulb's beaded chain and pry open the canister holding the reel for tomorrow night's first film. Movies are nothing but a bunch of acetate squares, and it's my job to connect the pieces, ready the stories to be lit. I splice in the previews, make sure one length leads correctly to the next. All around me, strips of film coil from hammered nails, reminding me of my mother's dark curls, spiralling from a wreath of daisy and baby's breath on her wedding day. Her dress had lace sleeves, a polyester skirt that fell to her ankles, and she looked happy, held by my father, whose smile was bracketed by bristling mutton chops. She was three months pregnant, but still slender.

The room is illuminated by a single forty-watt bulb, and because it's so dim I sometimes make mistakes. Once I spliced and assembled a film upside down; another time the movie was silent because I hadn't correctly threaded the strip that carries the sound. Usually I leave the door open to circulate the air and I like it when Frank appears in the dusty, wood-panelled hall-way, carrying a cigarette. The smoke drifts in with his voice or his chuckling laugh, and it's like we're sharing something that's only ours. He does that now, the two of us alone in the huge building, the floorboards creaking. Up close, he's layered with complex odours—that stale, sweet smoke, the musky smell of new cologne. I want to move closer, press my face against his chest. It isn't sex, it isn't that.

"You should have gloves on," he says.

"I can't feel it right," I tell him, expecting the same joke he usually makes—*no gloves, no love*—but he just watches as I feed the film into the tiny metal teeth. Only when I nick myself does he leave, walking away as I bring my finger to my lips to suck at the red bead. Sometimes blood smears on the smooth celluloid, showing up as scars on people's faces, shadows on calm water like creatures threatening to rise.

MY MOTHER AND FRANK used to date. This is a small town; things like that happen in small towns. They are both nearly twice my age, while my father was a few years older. He was a Hixon, my father, the eldest son of the owner of the sawmill that closed two years ago, after almost a century in business. When he was twenty, he crossed the border to join the fight in Vietnam. and my mother, who volunteered as a candy striper, met him when he came home, a hero to some, a traitor to others. The way she tells it, my father swayed her with his bravery as he healed in the hospital from shrapnel injuries and napalm burns. The backs of his hands were pouched and wrinkled, like part of him was older than the rest.

There were rumours when I was a kid that my father had blown his inheritance on a woman he met in Hanoi. In fact, he'd spent most of it buying back my mother's childhood home. Once, it had been the nicest house in town, a classic Queen Anne with fancy trim, but now the paint's flaking, gingerbread details are striated with rot.

One corner of the verandah is sinking, and the garden's overgrown with untamed roses, choking trumpet vine. A carpet of glossy periwinkle fills the huge yard that slopes to the shore. Every window looks out at the lake, except those on the north side, which are clotted with spiderwebs, some cracked and broken, frost quilting the interior panes in deep winter. Most of the rooms are filled with my mother's things: wrinkled cardboard boxes, out-of-fashion clothing, her expansive owl collection, and yellow newspaper clippings she's snipped out to read and claims to be cataloguing for a book on the town's history.

If I set my mind to it, I could go through all the junk and probably unearth my family history, a few items of value, but it's hard enough just to live there. Jonathan makes jokes about finding Miss Havisham, dressed in her rotting wedding gown, and I don't laugh, but my mother does. Not because it's funny. To show him that she's smart, that she appreciates a sharp intelligence, and Jonathan likes it. Jonathan listens to her when what passes for conversation is the delivery of facts, the offering of information about Hitler or the pyramids or whatever else she's learned from the History Channel. That's her role in life, I think: to teach these useless facts she assumes others do not know.

AT THE THEATRE, the next night, I can't concentrate. Jonathan was supposed to pick me up in my car and drive me to work. To take me for fish and chips at the marina like he'd promised when we spoke on the phone that afternoon. The clock on the kitchen stove ground closer to six before I realized I had to walk. When I finally arrived, Frank tapped his watch while I rushed upstairs to the reel room.

Slowly, I load the night's second film, fingers cramping. I double-check, then cut, attach the ends with slivers of tape. Frank keeps appearing in the doorway, aftershave stronger than the night before, and I ask him to eyeball my work, but he's gruff.

"Looks good," is all he says. Then he's gone.

At the concession stand, I burn the first batch of popcorn and count the float three times, each tally different. Frank's upstairs, setting up the reel, positioning his foot to control the quaking. Frustrated, holding a clutch of twenties, I stop and stare out through the window. Across the road is a supermarket. The green-and-white-striped awning, the gold lettering on the large window. They rent videos and VHS machines, too, and I watch a man carry one to his car, the black briefcase making him look like a KGB operative ferrying secrets down a shadowy Moscow street. Heading out on a mission.

IT'S LONG PAST midnight when Jonathan shows, pushing through the front doors. I glimpse my car through the blur of a hard rainfall, aimed the wrong way, parked crooked, with the driver's-side tire up on the curb.

"You drove?" I hiss as my fingers make change for a ten, sliding loonies and dimes out of the cash register. I drop the money in a girl's palm and watch her eyes scrape over Jonathan, who stands at the end of the counter, a stupid, damp grin on his face. She's in high school, and her friend presses against her, holding her elbow, as they stare at my drunk boyfriend. Their voices chime in unison. "Hi, Mr. Fielder."

Jonathan smiles, slurs a name, Cindy or Cynthia, before they push off, clutching each other, red liquorice fanned over giggling faces.

"Sit," I command, kicking the metal leg of a chair. Jonathan drops onto the wooden seat and lays his hands neatly on his knees as I finish with the last of the kids, some too young to have stayed for *Resident Evil*, but by then I don't care. When the room's emptied, I turn to him, find him sitting as if in an office, readying himself for a diagnosis.

When I hold out my hand for the keys, he stares at me, then thrusts his hands into his jacket pockets and grins. "Oops."

This has happened before. He's trained himself to flip the switch for the automatic lock on the driver's-side door, but when he's drunk he forgets that the keys are still in the ignition. I grit my teeth, close my eyes. When I open them, I see how he's pushed his hand against his lips and I think he's going to be sick, so I pick up a cardboard popcorn bucket, the biggest size, thrust it his way and wait. I'm seriously about to do it, to tell him it's over, I'm done, but before I can speak, he sucks a breath through his nose, pushes his hair off his forehead, and says, "I can't do this anymore."

My mouth falls open a bit, but he doesn't notice. He fumbles in his jacket's inner pocket and pulls out the flask, holds it loosely. I know now that the lettering spells *First Mate*, that it came from his father, a gift for his graduation just a few weeks before his dad dropped dead of a heart attack. He told me this on our second date, and I'd stopped eating, set down my fork, pressed my fingers against his sleeve. I was about to tell him about me, my story, when he asked if I wanted to get the cheque, pressed the cold flask against my bare knee under the table.

Now I stare at him, say, "You *can't*?"

He doesn't hear me right, doesn't hear my press on the first word, the sarcastic lilt, and actually thinks it's a question. His head wobbles side to side, eyelids drooping, so I think he's about to pass out. I slam the glass case that holds the chocolate bars, and his chin jerks up.

"No," he says. "This town…"

I keep closing up, mopping spilled butter, capping the plastic containers of sour keys and jujubes that sit on the counter. My movements angry, too aggressive for the subtle jiggle that's needed to work the lock that secures the cash cupboard, so the key jams.

He clutches his throat with one hand. "It's sucking me dry."

You, he means. *You*.

"Well, that's that then," I blurt, blinking hard so he can't see my tears. It's just another reminder, as if I needed one, that life isn't what I see here, at the theatre, not so easily plotted. All the inciting incidents in the world can't push me out of my mother's house, make me pack a bag, head to the city—Toronto, New York, even Sudbury—for a fresh start. That montage of scenes: my car stuffed with belongings, speeding down the highway; hands on my hips as I assess a squalid apartment I'll make into a home. A daub of paint on my nose, shopping for thrift store treasures, pushing through crowds to find work before gaining true love through some charming series of coincidences.

When Frank walks in, I'm surprised to see him because it means he's abandoned the rattling machine. The picture will be shivering, faces blurring, contorting into an abstraction, but he looks pleased with himself. He comes behind the counter to grab a rag, wipes the grease off his fingers. "Fixed it," he says. "Not out of a job yet."

"Can I go?" I ask. "Can you drive me home?"

"Des," Jonathan says.

Frank looks at him, then at me. He glances toward the the-atre, which is full of teenagers throwing popcorn across the seats, spilling sugary pop, making out. The way it's always been, the way it was when I was a kid. Suddenly I remember how Frank would snap on the house lights, even stop the reel, so we'd all freeze in that obtrusive blast of clear light, made aware we'd gone too far. My own face flushed, pulling back from the lips of some boy who'd eventually leave to study engineering or political science and never, ever come back, except occasion-ally for Community Days, showing up like a celebrity.

"Can he stay?" Frank asks, gesturing at Jonathan. We both look at him until he stands, steadying himself against the counter. Quickly, I grab my purse, my bag of knitting brought for the last long hour of the night, and walk into the lobby. Frank follows, his hand floating up behind me, briefly touching my lower back. I feel him, warm and reassuring, offering a grav-ity I want to sink into, be held by, secured in place. My bottom lip quivers and I swallow hard, shove my shoulder against the theatre's door to push outside.

"YOU OKAY?" Frank asks, as I look out the car window, fist pushed against my chin.

"Jonathan dumped me."

"Good riddance. You can do better than..."

His voice fades as he turns into my driveway. Every single light in the house is on, turning the windows into bright yellow boxes. My mother on a rampage, looking for something she thinks she's lost—a ceramic doll from her childhood, letters my father wrote to his sister during the war, the coroner's report that for a few weeks sat on her bedside table, under romance novels she refused to admit she read.

When I look over at Frank, his eyes are pinned to the front of the house. "Is it weird for you?" I ask. "To drop me off like this?"

Because of my mother, I mean. Because of how he would have brought her home, late, after a date. He would have done it right, I know: shut the car off, extinguished the headlights, held her elbow as he led her to the door that had been painted red for her sixteenth birthday. The colour now faded to a dim coral pink as if submerged underwater, affected by the murk.

My mother, thin then, would have been calm and assured with her pale, flawless skin, her black hair falling in a gleaming wave to her waist, her self-described sage-coloured eyes that are now often bloodshot, squinting out of the puffy flesh on her face. He would have leaned his handsome young face toward hers.

"Did you kiss her?" I whisper.

When he doesn't answer, I feel a tender, stinging burn in my cheeks.

The rain has slowed, nearly stopped, and the siding on our house looks milky where it isn't touched by the sulphuric haze of the street light. I imagine my face, lit yellow, the colour of amber, the shade of a shut-down liver.

"I should go," Frank says. "I should get back."

"I'm sorry," I say. "But I love—" When he interrupts me, I feel an instant, cold regret.

"No, you don't." His voice is blunt and he's fidgety. I can sense how much he wants to get away, his hands tightly gripping the cracked leather steering wheel of his old Cadillac like he's still driving, like we're going somewhere, taking that curving ocean highway into a happy ending. It's not unlike a game I used to play as a kid, in my father's rusting red truck, logs in front of the tires so I couldn't drive away by accident. Pretending.

Yes, I do, I think, although truthfully I'm not sure. All I know is I have this itch in me: to move, leap, see what will happen, crack open my life. I'm still young. I could have whatever I want, but when Frank sneaks his right hand over his lips to stifle a yawn, I realize I'm boring him. A pit of need yawns open inside me, hungry, hungry, and I pull the door handle because if I don't get out I'll only humiliate myself more. The light in the car springs on, blinding, and suddenly we are a bright island, a stage set, our own scene. Ahead of us, the green curtain in the dining room window drops.

He reaches out to touch my arm, and I stop, afraid but eager. Maybe this is it, I think, feeling the familiar rush of hope that surges in me, night after night. I stare ahead at the rock garden I'd razed and replanted in the spring, wanting growth, new green things. Nearby, there's a rusty swing set, a stack of aluminum lawn chairs whose woven ribbons have frayed into clots of orange strands.

"Life's long, and then you're forty," Frank says. "Fifty, sixty. So you should—"

"What?" I prod, wanting him to tell me, to give me clear instructions. But his cellphone rings, an old-fashioned jingling bell, and he fumbles for it, shuts off the ringer.

"Marie," he says. "My wife."

As if I don't know who she is. Wouldn't she be in bed though? Wouldn't she be sound asleep? Frank's gaze drops to the gearshift, then rises to the windshield, and he reaches forward to touch a chip in the glass from something, from a stone spat up on a gravel road, I think, bouncing past one of those old cabins you find in the woods. Abandoned, logs green with moss, wood stove lichened with rust, blackened tin cans with their paper labels chewed off by mice. A place like where they found my father after a two-day search. It was Frank who'd laid eyes on him first, knew who he was, knew his name. Dead of a gunshot wound. An accident, they said, but even at fifteen I knew that wasn't right.

IN THE MORNING, my mother asks me what I'm doing with Frank. It's early, just after eight, and I should be sleeping, but the CBC news woke me, its intro music playing loudly from the living room stereo. She's in her chair at the kitchen table, a smear of yellow yolk hardening on her breakfast plate beside a tiny pile of eggshells, her coffee cup marked by the crimson lipstick she puts on, repeatedly, throughout the day. A game of solitaire is spread in a clearing pushed into the clutter, and she draws three cards, smacks them down, repeats. Her fingers move a four of clubs to the matching pile.

"Nothing," I say, but my stomach writhes. I spit it out: "I think I want my own place. I think it's time."

My mother twists to look at me. She watches me as I wait for the kettle to boil on the stove. Her eyes are calculating, like she's trying to remember all the details she can, do the math about my existence: how old I am, my weight, the mark I got in Grade 12 chemistry, when I got my first period. I pull a tea bag out of the box, fingers trembling, ignoring her, but at the end of her assessment, she says, "You'd just leave me like that?" Her voice climbs into shrillness. "What kind of person are you?"

Staring down at the building wisps of steam, I don't answer, but I wonder, yes, what kind of person am I? I think about what Frank said, about how middle age is right around the corner, even though I can't yet see it.

"And Jonathan?" she asks, when I walk over to the table with my mug, take my usual seat. "Where is he?"

At the bottom of the lake, sleeping it off in the woods by the water tower—how am I supposed to know? I shrug.

"He's your boyfriend."

I make a *pff* sound with my mouth. Tea sprays. She exaggerates the task of wiping the backs of her cards on her pale pink robe, which is soiled with the grey rub of newspaper ink, dribbled soup.

"Keep that up, Desiree."

"Keep what up?"

"It's not very attractive is all."

Oh, I'm sorry, I think. I ram a crust of blackberry-jam-smeared toast from the edge of her plate into my mouth. *I guess I should go slip on my ball gown.*

Footsteps sound behind me. I turn sharply and see Jonathan climbing the basement stairs. He must have slept down there, sprawled on the couch like a vagrant. While I glare at him, wanting to tell him to leave, my mother's face beams, aimed like the shaft of light pouring out of the spinning projector.

"Speak of the devil," she says.

When he sits down, I stand. I'm seething. Had he stumbled up the hill, decided not to bother walking the rest of the way to his apartment, let himself in with our hidden spare key? *The fucking nerve,* I'm thinking, but all he says is, "Good morning," as if nothing's happened, like no decision was made. My mug clatters onto the counter and I spin away, pushing through the living room, through the quaking piles of cardboard boxes built into a maze, and out the front door.

I'M HALFWAY DOWN the hill, halfway to the intersection where the town's only street light stops traffic on the Trans-Canada so drivers can take a look around, wonder what it would be like to live here: the Legion with its patch of cigarette-butt-strewn grass, the hand-pencilled OPEN sign in the window of the Three Aces, the theatre with its slick roof needing reshingling, the dam blocking the river from the lake. I'm striding along the wet sidewalk, intent on sticking my thumb out to catch a ride east to Sudbury, or west to the Soo, farther still to Winnipeg, Moose Jaw, all the way to Vancouver, when I stop. I have no luggage, no money, not even a jacket. Moisture, almost imperceptible, is soaking into my clothes from the sodden grey sky.

BACK AT THE HOUSE, Jonathan has pushed aside a heap of cassette tapes and magazines and moved a cracked glass vase to the counter. He and my mother are silently playing gin rummy while the radio rumbles in the background, Lister Sinclair's voice saying something about Mozart that I don't really hear. His calming baritone washes over me like a father giving advice as I arrive in the kitchen intent on speaking, on saying something. Something about me, about what I want, my life. A fan of playing cards is veiling Jonathan's face, and my mother has her back to me. A familiar triangle of moles quivers on her neck as she lifts her left hand, aware of my presence, beckoning for service. I know exactly what she wants. I open the fridge for the milk.

Rhubarb

Josie's family came from Saudi Arabia when we were in Grade 4. She stood at the front of the class as the teacher introduced her, one hand cupping a bony elbow, and the ends of her long blond hair tangled like they'd been dipped in sugar. Her father had worked in the oil industry, we learned, and she'd gone to an American school, details too big for most of us small-town kids to quickly digest. In the school-yard, we watched as she wound her fingers through the chain-link and stared out at the lake, at the fishery's squat white boats motoring out and back in, seagulls accompanying them like kites. I wondered what it was like moving somewhere with so much water after a place with so much sand, but I didn't ask her or say anything about it to Sam and Lara as we whispered in a clutch by the gym door, beside the four-square. Gradually, we drifted over and encircled her, and she became one of us, her pigtails jumping in the blur of plastic pink rope.

When you're a teenager, you never want to think it, but by Grade 10 I pretty much figured we'd drift apart. Even though Sam talked about us having babies, renting summer cottages so our husbands could go fishing at dawn. *But Bruce Cartwright?* Lara would say when we were seventeen, and it was obvious it wouldn't work. Lara, with her nose ring and dragonfly tattoos, was out of place in that fantasy—the fridge chattering with beer bottles, the guys barbecuing bloody steaks while we did the dishes and handed out fruit-juice Popsicles to the kids.

Right after high school, Josie married Bruce Cartwright. Sam, Lara, and I sat at our table in shock as the drinks piled up into a smallish disaster. We were headed for university, and here was Josie, Bruce burrowing under her lace-and-polyester dress for the garter belt in the room above the hockey rink. Fake purple lilacs on the tables. Peas and carrots, mashed potatoes, turkey drying out in the chafing dishes.

Josie's parents paid for the wedding because they had money. We all knew that. Her dad worked as an executive at the uranium refinery and her mother was a home nurse. When they moved to town, they bought one of the new houses, half brick, half siding, on Concession Road. Lara and I would walk by sometimes, but we never dropped in unless we were invited. One spring Josie's mother planted a vegetable garden in the front yard, but we didn't see her outside, not once, and soon it was all a weed-clenched shambles, deflated orange tomatoes glowing on the lawn.

ON THE UPSTAIRS level of the market, Josie finishes her coffee and sets the empty mug on another table so the busboy can pick it up. I've still got most of mine because I like to drink it slow. I hold it with both hands while she picks at her half of a Texas doughnut, eating like a bird, choking down each crumb. With her free hand she plays with my car keys, with the peacock-feather key chain Lara sent me for my last birthday, when I turned thirty-five. Other than on Facebook, no one else remembered, but then my sister had a new baby and my parents were on a cruise and I hadn't really expected to hear from Sam.

I drove today, because Jo's car is on the fritz, a busted alternator she told me about on the way over, when she met me after school and we drove downtown. Now she's got this look on her face like the hard chocolate icing is way too sweet, and I'm waiting for her to confess whatever's bothering her, but she keeps talking about the house.

"There were tons of cops there," she says, meaning last August, a month before I moved back. A whole winter's passed since, and now the leaves are coloured the neon green of spring.

"The driveway was all clotted up with vehicles," Josie says. "Jammed in like a used car lot."

She tried to get a good shot of the haz-mat team coming out of the lab, but there were too many details crowded into her lens. When she moved, stepping backwards, the leaves of a gigantic rhubarb brushed against her bare calves. "Biggest I've ever seen," she says. Her spoon stabs the air between us, punctuating the thought. "It takes years to get that big."

Except for the part about the plant, I already know most of what she's saying from living in a small town, but I let Josie talk. She's the expert. She's the one who writes articles for the local paper, who stood on the road that summer day with her camera and took pictures of an officer hauling a man wearing studded leather pants and a red wife-beater through the front door. Arms behind his back, wrists bound by a plastic zip tie. When they let her on the property, the officers posed beside a pool table, its torn green felt heaped with guns, then escorted her into the Quonset hut so she could see the beakers, stripped batteries, residue-stained mason jars for herself.

That house has always been bad news, but when we were teenagers it was fun. The Donnelly family owned it. My mother, an English teacher at the Catholic high school, called them the Black Donnellys because the parents relocated to the Yukon for work and left the place in the hands of their sixteen- and eighteen-year-old kids. Every weekend there were parties. The cops were always showing up. Once, Lara rolled out a bedroom window and broke her wrist before the police could bust in and charge her with underage drinking. Usually I sat on the garage roof with others, sipping from a communal bottle of cherry whisky or lemon gin while we invented dialogue for films playing at the drive-in theatre across the field. Sometimes we'd watch in silence, aware of the prickle of heat between our knees as the giants kissed. We all wanted that, especially those of us on the garage roof and not in the back bedroom before the waterbed broke or downstairs on the basement couch. Those characters found love while we lined the rooftop like ravens, looking for something shiny to steal. In the years between then and now: biker gangs, drug busts, city hookers haunting the doorway at 3:00 a.m. Everything's changed.

"It's such a waste," Josie says, licking chocolate off her fingertip, and I think of her mother's old garden: spiky arugula gone to seed, zucchinis swelling into oblong balloons, woody, not worth harvesting. "Tomorrow's Saturday," she tells me.

My spare room is still full of boxes, and I was planning to spend the day unpacking, although I know what that means: that I'm staying, settling in, attempting to coexist with the awkward shadow of my youth. It's sticky, that shadow. Everywhere I go, it fastens to me, like a piece of toilet paper dragging on my heel. I shift in my seat.

"Why didn't you get it right then? Ask to dig it up and bring it home?"

She shrugs one shoulder in that exaggerated way, a forward roll like her muscles are aching and she's trying to stretch them out. Her body curves around her centre. "They wouldn't let me. Then winter came and I kept thinking about it." She spreads her left hand on the table. "I guess it's stupid," she says, staring at the miniature glitter of her ring.

I swallow the last of my double-double and don't respond. Josie usually needs reassurance, but I've never heard her talk like this: so sad about something that seems so small. Her voice is whiny when it comes again.

"Now Bruce says I can't use the truck."

"Asshole," I mutter.

Josie looks up. "People don't realize how stressful it is to be an electrician."

When I don't respond, she pushes the last of her doughnut away and asks if I want to see a movie—*Ratatouille*—playing at the Palace. I don't want to. It's a kids' movie and I know how it will be: the theatre overrun with adolescents on dates, calling across the audience, their sneakers suctioning to the sticky floor as they run up and down the aisles. That's what it was like for us: popcorn thrown over the heads of adults who didn't realize the place was ours. Now I'm one of those adults.

"WHAT ARE YOU doing there?" Lara asks me on the phone that night.

I'm drunk on a single bottle of wine, sitting on the cold, cracked tile of the bathroom floor. I shove a hand into my hair, hold it back from my face. "Where are you?" I ask.

"At home."

I hear her smoking, the inhale and exhalation, and imagine her analyzing one of her paintings, figuring out what colour it needs as smoke curls against the ceiling.

I always thought I was right behind her, that I'd send Josie a few letters from university, meet up with her for lunch when I came back home at Christmas, but that my experiences would be too thrilling for her to understand, even though it was she who'd travelled into our circle from the most exotic place we could once imagine. Life is funny though. University led to teachers college to several years supply teaching in the city before I finally got a contract teaching Grade 5. It happened to be back home. My parents aren't here anymore—they moved south after my sister left for college—so Josie let me stay with her and Bruce before I found my own place. He was okay but unpredictable, either cracking jokes or so withdrawn it seemed he was only half there. One night he backhanded a bowl of olives across the kitchen. Purplish brine all over the wall, a spackling of red-pepper flakes.

"I don't remember him like that," I said to Josie that night, after he left, trying to comfort her. In Grade 10, drunk, Bruce had kissed Lara during the last song of the Hawaiian dance and then refused to talk to her the next day when she called him. The summer before Grade 12, he and Josie hooked up at a house party and slept together on a trampoline in the backyard. Afterward, they lay there for a long time, affecting each other with their smallest movements. It sounded romantic to me back then, but I always remembered Lara rolling her eyes.

I see he's still a jerk, Lara wrote back when I told her about the olives in a text.

"Seriously, Mel," she says now.

My voice gurgles up. "I don't have a choice. Go where the work is. Do you know how hard it is to find a contract?"

"Yeah, yeah."

Probably she's right. I could have gone anywhere—a fly-in reserve in Northern Manitoba, China, maybe even Saudi Arabia. "I don't know," I say, and at that moment the train whistle blows, a lonely siren north of town. It's the sound that punctuated our childhood. "Hear that?"

"Yeah," she says. "It just gave me the heebie-jeebies."

"Why don't you come for a visit?" I ask like I do almost every time. She doesn't say no, but I hear the groan of distance, five hundred kilometres of forest and lakes, and the rock of the Canadian Shield heavy between our words.

THE HOUSE is a split-level with grubby yellow siding covered in scrawls of red graffiti: *guvernmint off our land, cops r pigs.* Dead yellow grass clots the front yard. The abandoned Toyota that kids used to make out in sits beside the dirt driveway, hood popped, and I can't believe it's still there. Years marked by a fringe of crumbling rust on the wheel wells, the web of the shattered windshield.

It's dusk, nearly dark, and we've driven in over the collapsed yellow crime-scene tape. The investigation into the biker gang is ongoing, Josie's told me, although the paper just gets the stories from the wire service now, so she no longer has the inside scoop. It's old history. We're trespassing, I know that much, but Josie doesn't seem to care. I haven't seen her so bold in years, although I know she'd never be here if I hadn't agreed to come. Sleeping with Bruce at that party was probably the most daring thing she's ever done.

We park facing the Quonset hut. "Was that even there back then?" I ask.

"That's where Luke built his model airplanes," says Josie.

The older brother. The hum of a WWII replica bomber diving into a circle of smoking teenagers.

"Who'd ever heard of meth back then," Josie says, as she opens the car door, but I remember plenty of cocaine, miniature ridges piling up on math and science textbooks, fat novels for English class like *Fifth Business* and *A Canticle for Leibowitz*.

My flashlight jumps over the ground, shines on the silver chain-link fence the bikers installed. When Josie shouts, *"There!"* I have to reverse direction and follow her pointing finger with the beam. She squats down, brushes the earth with her searching fingers, and looks up at me, smiling.

The rhubarb seems impossibly young. Tiny, wizened leaves that look like brains, stalks sprouting from a tissuey pocket that's fleshy and pink. Against the dun-coloured earth, the plant is vibrant red, like part of a human being pushing out of the ground. We crouch on either side. Josie strokes the edges of the small, bumpy leaves. "I thought you said it was big," I say.

"They die away over winter."

I'm surprised by her knowledge. I'm not a gardener myself and her mother seemed to fail miserably. We're ready with the cardboard box and the spade, and really I just want to get moving. I spent the afternoon unpacking things I realized I could have lived without and feel tired.

Josie stabs the shovel into the ground. She tries to lift the whole thing, but the plant tugs against her. "Huge root system," she says, and starts again, piercing the blade deeper until she can scoop it all out: a bucket-sized clump of earth and those red stalks, almost unrecognizable as a plant, a thing that will actually grow.

When we slide it into the trunk of my car, Josie lays the spade down and says, "What now?"

"You should get that in the ground."

"Don't you want to see what's playing? "

Across the field, the screen of the drive-in movie theatre is darker than the surrounding sky. It shut down last fall. "Like, pretend," Josie says, her voice small. The gleam in her eye pleads silently.

There's a stepladder leaning against the Quonset hut. Even from outside I can smell the chemical stench: sharp, like cat urine and rotten eggs. We move the ladder over to the garage, but it's too short, so we have to pull ourselves up, hands gripping the edge of the asphalt shingles, knees swinging sideways to crawl onto the slope. When I was sixteen it was a lot easier, and when we reach the top, we're both out of breath, but Josie is giggling. Car lights slide by on the highway, and I watch them nervously, as if expecting my mom and dad to show up. But it isn't that. Instead I'm thinking about my kids' parents, what would happen if Officer Gagnon, whose son is in my class, came.

Carefully, Josie pulls two cigarettes out of her jacket. "I never came up here," she says, rolling them in her fingers so I can smell the minty aroma.

"Yes, you did," I say, although I know she's right. Usually she was in the house, her body encircled by an arm—Bruce's or, before him, another guy's. Kevin, then James. I take one of the cigarettes even though I want to refuse.

"Found these in Bruce's truck," Josie says.

"Menthol?" I ask as she inhales hard, as if hungry, and lets the peak of the roof support her.

"Head rush," she says.

I light mine but don't suck the smoke into my lungs, at least not at first. Then it's like something hard and adult abandons me, and I lean back, loosened, and laugh. After a minute she starts telling me about the rhubarb pies she'll make, how we'll lick our plates for the last of the sweet, gummy pulp. When she stops talking, there's a silence between us because I'm not sure what to say. It isn't the same, sitting up there, only the two of us. I miss Lara. I look across the field at the empty screen, and suddenly Josie sits up like she's remembered something important.

"We should start it up again," she says. "Get a loan. Do it all old-fashioned with 1950s intermission movies and shit like that."

"Hmmm," I say.

"I mean it."

"I have a job," I tell her, and toss my burning cigarette over the edge.

BRUCE ISN'T HOME, but Josie doesn't say anything about it. I carry the box into their backyard and watch in the wash of yellow from the sensor lights as she digs a hole beside her immaculate garden. The new tomato plants are a fragile green blur inside their clear plastic domes. She lowers the plant, soaks it with the hose, then pushes the earth back in. Gently, she pats down the dirt and sits back on her heels. The forest circling her yard is dark and quiet, and when she stands and wipes her hands on her jeans, I remember us building forts back there, eating cucumber-and-mayonnaise sandwiches under the cedars, imagining our lives. We're so still that the lights go out, and Josie waves her arms to turn them on like a shipwreck survivor who's seen a boat.

Inside, we have a few glasses of wine and watch a couple episodes of *Lost* burned on a DVD. We don't really talk. It's late so I stay over, on the blow-up mattress in the room Josie's still hoping will be a nursery, although they've been trying for years. In the dark, I lie there wondering when it will happen, if it will, and am filled with sudden longing. Only Sam has a baby, a girl Josie and I met over the Christmas holidays mostly because Sam wanted to show off. We held her at Sam's parents' place out at the lake, in the den where we used to have slumber parties. I can't sleep, so I text Lara, but she doesn't answer. Out, probably, at some glamorous gallery opening or late-night poetry reading, although I know that really she's probably asleep.

IN THE MORNING, I leave before Josie wakes up. I drive to both grocery stores before I find what I'm looking for: a strawberry-rhubarb pie—frozen, but it'll do. The driveway is still empty when I get back, and Bruce isn't home by the time Josie pads out to the kitchen in her rabbit slippers. Her nose is up, exaggeratedly sniffing the smell of hot sugar filling the house.

When she pushes her fork into the pastry, it's tough, like cardboard, like the many boxes I emptied of my things the day before and collapsed for recycling. She scrapes the pink filling off the bottom slab and piles it on the plate's rim.

"I can do better," she says when the truck finally rumbles up the driveway. She reaches down and cinches the belt of her housecoat.

"I know," I tell her, remembering the raspberry-chocolate birthday cake she made for her own party the spring she turned sixteen. Outside, a vehicle door slams, and I stand up. Josie prods the crust, her face tight. I squeeze her shoulder. "Call you later," I say, but she doesn't answer.

BRUCE STALLS when he sees me. Hands in his pockets, scraping the toe of one untied work boot over the crushed gravel. After a minute, as if we're still in high school, he says, "What'd you girls do last night?"

I think about telling him. I know Josie will. But I also know what'll happen—how cool he'll find it, how he'll be over at the house with his buddies and who knows who else, breaking in through the back door, wandering room to room, reminiscing. Beers out, then the 26ers, and then the partying like no time at all has passed.

"You should just break up with her," I blurt out, as if we aren't adults, as if they haven't been married for fifteen years. "Just let her go."

He nods once. I can tell he doesn't know how else to answer.

As I pull away, he stands in the driveway, probably too nervous to go inside. He shrinks in my rear-view mirror until he's no larger than a figurine, one of those tiny brown ceramic animals that used to come in tea boxes that Josie's grandmother collected. I think about the stolen plant in Josie's backyard. Those wrinkled green leaves fanning open, the rosy limbs thickening with bitter sugars. How big it will get, how soon.

Empty Nest

ara's brother disappeared in late August. He packed his things—tent, blue tarp, a coil of yellow rope burned black at both ends—and walked into the woods behind their house. He was wearing the expensive Gore-Tex jacket his parents had bought him for his birthday, both feet wrapped in plastic bags inside his boots. It wasn't supposed to rain, but he was like that. Prepared.

On Sunday, his boss from the Esso station up the highway stopped by to see why he'd skipped work that morning, and Lara's parents got worried. The police came. A search party. Border collies panting through the woods while a helicopter shook the treetops. A hard downpour had soaked the spruce and thick cedar, so moving in the forest was like digging through clothing dredged up from the lake. For two and a half weeks, they looked, found nothing.

THE BUS WE TOOK to the high school picked Lara up near Serpent River, then came west on the highway to wind through my subdivision, drive on into town. In September, I sat beside her on the hard green seats, picking at a kid's carved initials in the vinyl above my kneecaps. That lasted the first few mornings, while they were still looking for Pete, and then I didn't see her on the bus anymore.

She was hitchhiking, it turned out, and this was scary. Since we were kids, Sam, Josie, Lara, and I had known that anybody could be driving that highway, heading from Toronto to Winnipeg or Vancouver, for all sorts of dark reasons. But she lived nearly an hour east of town and her parents only had one car, I said, making excuses to the other two. They were gone all the time, too, meeting with police or reporters at the newspaper or their church prayer circle that Lara told me about in snide tones. She yelled a lot those days, about stupid things: how much she hated Sam's penchant for pink cardigans or the misogynist rap music at the Donnellys'. One Saturday night in early October, she shut the music off and the sharp click of the ghetto blaster button initiated a silence that stopped the party. Lara stood chest-to-chest with Adam, the big guy whose music it was, while Sam, Josie, and I watched, strangling the necks of our beer bottles. At the same time, Shannon and Jig, the two goths, moved in to side with Lara. All three of their faces powdery white, eyelashes clotted with mascara. Lara's short blond hair dyed black by then, capping her head like crow feathers.

"Freaks," Sam hissed, and I could smell the sourness of her breath, felt it damp against my cheek. I pushed it off my skin.

The music came back on. Everything returned to normal, but that was when I knew for sure, right then, that Lara was no longer ours.

It wasn't a smooth break though. In high school it hardly ever was. There was shame involved in the rupture of a friendship, so for a little while she still tried and so did I. Late at night, usually when I was already in bed, she would call me. I could tell it was her by the cooing sweetness of my mother's voice through the wall, and I'd get up, walk to the phone in the kitchen, scream "I got it!" into the hush of the house.

"GOOD RIDDANCE," Sam said the Monday after the Donnellys' house party, at lunch. She sucked up the last of her Diet Coke. We were sitting on the rickety wooden bleachers that surrounded the gravel track. Half a mile away, Lara, Shannon, and Jig stood in a cluster by the riverbank boat launch like some sort of strange animal herd.

Josie dragged a French fry through a pond of gravy in the foam container on her lap.

"I don't feel like that," I said.

Sam dropped her empty pop can, crushed it against the earth with her dusty penny loafer.

"What are we supposed to do?" said Josie through the mash of potato in her mouth. She held her fingers over her lips as she talked.

"People grow apart," said Sam.

I knew that was true, but we'd been friends for most of our lives. There were ties, not just stupid linear history, but a dense tangle. We'd known each other since we were small children; we were falling together from the nest.

I watched Lara, who was dressed in black-and-white-striped tights under a short black skirt and one of her many new tops coloured charcoal, jet, onyx, midnight. Smoke drifted out of their circle. She had her back to us, as if afraid to let us see.

That morning in the hallway she'd walked right by my locker, staring straight ahead like I was invisible, pointy stars sketched in eyeliner on both of her cheeks. Had our friendship been a living thing, she would have killed it that autumn. Caught it, wrung its neck, put it out of its misery. If I hadn't been protective, built a cage around it, tried to keep it safe.

"She's had a hard time," I muttered.

We sat there, thinking about Pete, or so I assumed until Sam leaned forward and half-whispered, "Bruce saw her get out of a transport the other day."

I SUPPOSE I WANTED to understand her, thought I was the only one who could, because on a Tuesday, in the middle of that fall, when the late bus dropped me off after band practice, I pretended to tie my shoe until the highway emptied. Instead of walking into our subdivision, I headed east along the Trans-Canada, kicking at loose stones as dusk gathered around the tops of the pine trees. My parents were away, had gone to Owen Sound to help my great-aunt move into a nursing home, and my sister was at her figure-skating lessons.

Two cars and a transport passed me before I got up the nerve to turn and face the traffic. Lara must not have been as scared as me, I thought. She never seemed afraid, always acted like some sort of Joan of Arc, clad in a uniform of clanking, dented armour, her pale face glowing through the grille, eyes lit, fiercely searching for justice.

The person who picked me up, who set a whole other thing in motion, was Mr. Decker. A few years ago, I'd babysat for him and his wife before they went through a spectacular divorce, all his clothes cut into pieces on their front lawn, the two of them screaming at each other on the main street. After that she'd moved north to Kirkland Lake to live with her sister. His long, cream-coloured Cadillac ambled to the side of the road and he leaned over, popped up the lock. When I didn't move right away, he stretched his arm farther, pushed open the door.

"Get in," he said, through the gap, his eyes tipped up to peer at me. The seat upholstery was burgundy, a shade of deep wine, and looked like crushed velvet from outside the car.

NOT LONG AFTER that day, Lara left. On the Monday after Halloween she just wasn't there. It was like with Pete, another vanishing. Josie, Sam, and I walked around, afraid, my heart a hot fist in my throat as rumours slid through the hallways: trucker abduction to runaway-turned-circus-freak. I hadn't told anyone about Decker, but I really wanted to tell her. Finally, Josie's mother talked to a friend of Lara's parents. "She's living with her aunt and uncle in Saskatchewan," Josie said on Friday morning.

"Where the hell is that?" said Sam.

I couldn't tell if she was joking. I remembered film reels clattering into the classroom silence in Grade 8. Scenes of flat land covered in swaying wheat stalks and bright yellow canola fields that I imagined Lara stepping through in her scuffed Doc Martens. She'd been dressing like that for only a couple months, but already I couldn't see her any other way.

"Things got out of hand," Josie said, arms clutched around her waist, leaning forward on the bleachers. The grass inside the track was white with hoarfrost. "Did you know she was carrying a knife? She used it on a guy who tried to drive her out to the copper mines. She came home with blood all over her, and her mom spazzed out."

"What happened to the guy?" Sam asked.

"Dead, probably," Josie said, her head turning to the river. It was inky-blue, still flowing.

"As if," said Sam.

SNOW CAME. The red and amber leaves along the river shook loose, leaving behind skinny black stick figures with arterial limbs. Slowly, the water froze. By December, I felt sure Lara would never be back. In my mind I saw her: a dark speck within a huge, blizzard-covered landscape, like the snow planet in *Star Wars*. Lost.

At Christmas, things seemed different between Josie, Sam, and me. Over the holidays, we hardly talked. We were like a spiderweb with one side ripped out, all of us hanging on despite the damage, thinking about rebuilding.

Early in the New Year, I called Lara's house. I'd heard that her parents had been out west to see her. Lara's mother's voice surprised me, how breathy it was, how hoarse, as if she'd completely dried out inside. She cleared her throat. "The prairies," she croaked. "So dry." She forced out Lara's new address, bit by bit.

MY LETTER WASN'T MUCH, just chatty. I thought about writing out what had happened, but it seemed too big a confidence to put in writing. Instead, I told her about Sam's party, where a basketball had smashed through her parents' glass coffee table and how Josie had failed her driver's test because she turned the wrong way down our town's only one-way street.

I felt nervous when I licked the stamp, wondering where the letter was going, if it would end up crumpled and in flames or hidden for all time in a tin mailbox on an abandoned dirt road. What I wrote meant nothing, I knew, next to what she was going through, what her journal entries must have looked like, but I didn't know what else to do. I waited. Unlocked the small steel box at the post office every afternoon and peered inside. These days it would be immediate: friendship or not, instant through the bright glare of a smart phone, *go away* jabbed out in a text. Then, my small i's were dotted with tiny stars and hearts so what I wrote had a kind of animated pleading.

WHEN DECKER PULLED out onto the road that day, he didn't check his blind spot. A horn screamed, and a car leaned hard into the other lane to swerve around us. The driver stuck his arm out the window to give us the finger, but Decker ignored him. There was a can of Coke in the cup holder between us, and I smelled the sweet treacle of alcohol in the air.

"Want some?" he asked, as the other car disappeared up ahead over the hill.

I shook my head. My hands were curled in my lap; my backpack, full of the math homework I had to do, and the novel *Flowers for Algernon*, which I needed to read, sat on the floor between my feet. Decker leaned back, left leg splaying toward the door. He had on jeans, a pink golf shirt, and his arms were nicely muscled, his stomach almost flat. Back when I was twelve, I'd had a crush on him, like most of the girls. Lara called him Officer Decker, then just Decker. He was one of the policemen who used to come to our school, clad in full uniform, the lump of a gun on his hip, to talk about stranger danger, being safe around frozen water. I didn't know if he still did that. He still wore his wedding ring. It shone against the dark leather of the steering wheel.

"Where you headed?" he asked, as if what I was doing was real.

"Serpent River," I said. "Near there."

He glanced at me, squinting in concentration. Outside, the blue of the sky was fading quickly to an ugly grey. "You're the sister," he said.

He had me confused. His eyes flashed between the road up ahead and my face until finally he lifted his hand off the steering wheel, finger wagging. A grin, that loose, sneaky one, the one I'd seen several times when he and his wife came home late and he lurched around the kitchen. He'd make a toasted tuna fish sandwich, draw pickles out of the brine with scissoring fingers, while Mrs. Decker pulled bills out of her wallet to give to me, lips ratcheted tight in annoyance.

"No," he said. "You're the girl, the one who looked after Libby."

I started to ask how she was—a little kid by then, no longer a baby—but he lifted the pop can to me, right up in front of my face so all I had to do was lean forward, rest my lips on the rim. I took a small drink. It burned like antiseptic on a cut.

LARA DIDN'T ANSWER my letter. Not for a long time. Not for months. After a while I only ever thought about her when she appeared in a dream, and that was when my dad brought home a postcard. "I think this is from your friend," he said. "With the brother…"

My mother shot him a look that seemed anguished, a superstitious second of fear.

It was a picture of beautifully painted eggs. Three of them in a scraggly straw nest, the shells painted with ornate designs. Curls and cross-hatched lines circled two blue-winged geese. A tiny woman in a wide skirt. A spiralling green snake. I flipped it over and read the word *pysanky* in black type above Lara's scrawl. *Ukrainian Easter Eggs.* All that beauty to shield the vulnerable inner space. *It's empty here but not flat,* Lara had written. *Hills, rivers, trees. Freezing fucking cold. No guys. Nothing to do. P.S. I'm coming home.*

WINTER WAS NEARLY OVER. Heaps of grey snow lay on the sidewalks like discarded dirty clothing. Josie came to school one day and told us her mother knew that Lara had returned, that she'd been back for a couple weeks, and why. Her eyes were big, so wide she looked like a little kid again, and for a second I was back in the schoolyard across town by the fishery, the four of us playing double dutch and chanting.

"They found him," Josie said, and told us about it in a whisper: how Pete was down a deep chasm, caught in an open seam of rock.

Sam started to cry, like he'd been her best friend.

It turned out that animals had tried to tug his body out during the winter, so a couple of men flagging a prospecting claim saw his fingers sticking out of the granite. At first they thought he was waving for help, but close up they saw the condition of his body.

There wasn't a funeral. Not much of one. A small gathering. Pete's ashes buried next to his grandparents.

ONE SUNDAY, out of the blue, Lara called. "What are you doing?"

I swallowed, searched for words, and finally just answered her question: "Nothing."

"I've got to get out of here."

"Okay."

I didn't know what I would say. At school we talked about Pete as if he were still alive: *So he was down there all winter? Just a few miles away?* Like he'd been waiting the whole season, bored silly, and had only recently succumbed.

My parents had taken my sister to Sudbury for a skating tournament, which was lucky because I wasn't sure how my mother would act, if she'd pile her hands on Lara's shoulders, make her a plate of cinnamon toast, not leave her be. I thought up five questions I could ask to get her talking and help me hold everything together. As soon as we went to my room, I started the script.

"So, did you do any farming out there?"

She looked at me funny. "Do you have any food?"

We went to the kitchen, and I peeked at her while I opened the cupboards. Her face was still pale, but not from any makeup I could see. Her hair was blond again and she wore the clothes she always had but with a few changes: the black-and-white tights peeked through the torn knees of her otherwise normal jeans. Light mascara set off the red in her bloodshot eyes.

In the kitchen, I poured Rice Krispies into two bowls, added milk, and shoved the sugar bowl across the table. The snap-crackle-pop filled the silence. Lara didn't touch her spoon. The cereal was growing soggy, and I hated it like that, but I got up and pressed Play on the tape deck in the living room. It was Casey Kasem's Top 40 from two weeks earlier, the long-distance dedication. "Say You, Say Me." Lara stuck her finger in her mouth.

"Do you know the Violent Femmes?" she asked. I shook my head and turned to shut off the tape. "Leave it," she said, so I left the music to play.

Eventually she started talking. She told me about the northern lights and about volunteering in her aunt's Grade 2 class, where the kids put their coats and scarves in designated cloth bags because of the lice. Bears were always standing on the edge of the highway, along the wall of black spruce. The pickerel her uncle caught were so big they barely fit through the holes he drilled in the ice. At night, she said, wolves howled from stands of diamond poplar.

All these details fell out of her before she got to what she really wanted to say. How the police had come by so her parents could identify Pete's things: the Gore-Tex jacket, his Swatch watch, all sealed in heavy plastic. The smell still there: the sweetest, deepest rot. Her mother had covered her face, held on to her head, and shuffled over to the couch to lie down like her bones were coming apart. Nothing had yet reattached.

Lara wasn't crying. The cereal grew quiet. I stared into it, wondering how long it would take before the milk would curdle. I had barely known Pete. He was bold and big, older. Like Decker, in a way. A man, comfortable in his body, aware of what he wanted. This spring, he would have finished his second year at York University in Toronto.

Pictures filled my brain. Of Pete, of course, but also the prairie she'd described, spotted with islands of trees and animals, veined with rivers. It made me think of the estuary my dad had taken us to the summer before, where the French River meets Georgian Bay and the Shield erupts out of the ground and it's like the earth has shattered and your boat is moving through all this rubble. It couldn't be anything like that, I knew, but was it?

Lara looked at the time on our stove. "I've got to go," she said.

My parents weren't back, so Lara called her house, and her father told her he couldn't come, that she was stuck with me for a while. "Don't hitch," I heard his far-off voice say through the phone, but I could tell she was itching to leave from the way she shuffled her feet under the table, pinching closed a hole in her white sock with her toes, then letting it flap open, her nail polish a sudden, sparkly blue.

DECKER HAD TAKEN me to his hunt cabin. Plywood walls, cobwebs clotted in the corners of the windows, a double bed covered in a sleeping bag that felt slippery and cold under my fingertips. He lit a fire in the pot-bellied stove, and we watched the orange flames through a crack in the open iron door until he lifted his hand to gently touch my neck, my jaw.

Earlier, we had stopped at the side of the road, at the trailhead near the steaming rapids, to look through the car windows at the bouquets of flowers and soggy cards that people from town, from Lara's church, had left in a heap through the fall. They were covered in a thin layer of snow, and the blossoms were breaking apart.

"Terrible thing," he muttered, and tears pooled in my eyes. I felt something reaching from down deep inside me, a desire I didn't understand, to stretch into the unknown, to grasp whatever it was that had disappeared or hadn't yet come to form.

THE THURSDAY AFTER she came to my house, Lara finally sat with us at lunch. She showed up, slid her brown tray onto the table beside Josie, and dropped into a chair. On the far side of the room, Jig and Shannon stood in the doorway, rolling cigarettes in their fingers to carry outside, their kohl-blackened eyes aimed at Lara. She ignored them, nibbling on a chicken salad sandwich just like she'd done in Grade 6. Eventually the girls left. I felt sorry for them but not enough to encourage Lara to go. I saw how her gaze followed their backs. She wanted out there still, I could tell.

None of us knew what to say. When Josie spoke, her voice was full of questions. "That movie's playing this weekend? The one with Christian Slater?"

"I love him," said Sam.

"You love everyone," said Josie.

"Everyone with a dick," said Lara, and Josie laughed awkwardly, like it was expected.

I saw the egg in her teeth, spotted with green parsley. The feet on Sam's chair screamed against the floor tiles as she shifted away hard. I set down the remaining crust of my ham sandwich, wondering how it was going to work now, when all these gusts had sent us apart.

"There's that video dance in Elliot Lake," Josie said.

Lara rolled her eyes. "Like, Huey Lewis in the Nude?"

"Come on," I said to Lara. "I can drive."

Lara picked up a chunk that had fallen from Josie's lunch. She set it on the edge of my tray, smeared the greasy yolk off her fingertip. "Maybe," she said.

"Don't do us any favours," said Sam.

"I won't." Lara looked out the high windows at the shuffle of feet in desert boots and high-top runners. Cigarette butts sparked on the ground as they fell.

OUTSIDE, AFTER LUNCH, on the mushy spring grass, in the middle of the track, I pulled out pieces of bread and threw them into the air for the seagulls. They closed around us like a blizzard. Their yellow talons hung down, nearly scratching Lara's forehead like she was something they wanted to carry away. Sam and Josie sat on the lowest bench of the bleachers and watched. I felt the wind from the flapping wings on my face, and when we all went inside to stand in a row at the washroom sinks, Lara's and my cheeks were flushed red like when we were little after skipping, after Capture the Flag, like after sex. The mirror held our eyes as they met, blurred at the edges from years of scratched initials, flowers with fat petals, an angular, angry heart.

Stories

Jonathan teaches English at the high school. His class-room is in one of the portables set up beside the outdoor basketball court, the garage where the guys in auto shop fix cars. During Grade 12 drama, I spent a lot of time in there with Mr. Chen, who came from the city and who Lara thought was gay. Once he told me to "stop acting so soap opera" and get the hair out of my face. Until then I thought it was a gift how I could make myself weep by remembering our cat Smiley, who died the winter I was eleven, who my dad wrapped in a plastic grocery bag and put under the strawberries in the chest freezer until the ground thawed enough to bury him. "Save your tears," Mr. Chen told me, and to this day, whenever I feel like I'm going to cry, his clipped, scolding voice comes into my head.

The classroom looks different now. Jonathan's covered the walls with movie-sized posters of Shakespeare performances at Stratford and pictures he's drawn and laminated that teach basic grammar rules: a bright red x over ITS' like the word is akin to smoking. I don't understand my apostrophes, but I don't tell him that. Possession isn't a topic I want to bring up.

I first noticed Jonathan at a PD day seminar in Sudbury, but really we met at the bar. I was out with Josie and we were sitting on the ladies' and escorts' side, cracking peanuts, dropping the shells on the floor. Her nose running, a tremble in her bottom lip. Earlier that week, on Wednesday, she and Bruce had had a fight over whether she should put garlic in her beef stew, and he'd taken a room at the Lakeshore. I was trying to listen, shoving slim paper serviettes across the table, guzzling from my Canadian because she preferred coolers and didn't want to split a pitcher. Through the row of windows overlooking the river, I could see the moon, a bright orb that lit the wide white plain. Divorce, I heard her say, and a flare of hope erupted in my chest, but right then headlights jumped up the shore into the parking lot and that was how he arrived: in a jumble of guys climbing off their sleds to enter the gentlemen's half of the bar. Our eyes immediately caught, and when I went to order more drinks, he came up to the heavy wooden counter that stretched the width of the building like the middle bridge of an H, linking the two sides together, and asked me my name. Josie's damp eyes stayed on me until finally I invited him over. When she turned to him, I saw her face flicker open with the slightest shaky smile.

JONATHAN IS WRITING a novel. Sometimes when I let myself into the house he bought up the hill from the high school, beside the water tower where the kids carpet the bare rock with the glittering amber dust of bottles, I hear the keys of his computer steadily clacking. While he works, I make him dinner, and occasionally he reads me bits of what he's written as we eat. I don't cook anything special: pasta and hamburgers, a meatloaf or casserole, mostly meals with ground beef or canned tuna. Josie is the one who took to that when we were kids, and I still love getting a dinner invitation from her because you never know what you'll have: beef bourguignon that took six hours, a Moroccan lamb stew with mint jelly, and always a special dessert, key lime pie or a sherry trifle, no matter the occasion.

THE FIRST NIGHT we met, Jonathan and I fucked. That's what he calls it, the sharp consonants percussing on his lips. Josie left early, drove home in her half-broken-down Honda, even though in the bathroom, I told her I'd do whatever she wanted. Go home or stay. The glare of the fluorescents revealed the splotchy weakness of grief in her face, the first lines around her eyes like pins hemming a skirt, and I thought, *We're too young for this*. Drunk enough, I hugged her, and I think that was when she decided just to leave.

Jonathan took me home on the back of his machine. I left my car in the parking lot. He went fast, and the wind bit at my earlobes, pressed easily through the denim skin of my jeans, but apart from all the beer, I'd done a few warming shots of cinnamon schnapps and the whole situation made me laugh. It seemed grandiose, an unusual adventure, a story to tell Lara the next time we talked on the phone.

As soon as we got through his front door, we did it. Right there in the living room, on the worn carpet, beside a stack of books I kicked over halfway through, hearing the tumble of their hard covers as if from a distance. Jonathan came, collapsed, and went suddenly so quiet that I thought he might have died or gone instantly to sleep and I would be stuck there until the morning, pulling thin breaths beneath his significant weight, patches of my bare skin growing numb.

I TELL JONATHAN my stories. He is fascinated that I grew up in Hixon River. We go out with Josie or over to her house, and he draws the words out of us, standing up from the dining room table like a gentleman, refilling our wineglasses, stopping any drips with that final, professional twist of the neck. In the attentive heat of his eyes, I feel alive and love when he gets so excited that he pulls out his tiny, leather-bound notebook and starts jotting things down. It's like a dare, that pen taking dictation, like a reporter inviting deeper and deeper intimacies, so Josie and I go further, telling all our tales about the four of us, Sam, Lara, she, and I, until finally he stops. He shakes his sore wrist, fingers flashing like a wing in full flight, and sits back, smiling his defeat. He can't keep up. We laugh. Somebody pours more wine, and Josie asks about his own childhood, spent down in Scarborough, in a suburb behind a mall. I act like I'm listening when I'm actually thinking about later, how I'll pretend not to want to and then let him, let him do whatever he wants.

WHEN THE LITERARY journal arrives in the mail, he tells me he's won third place. "The Tar Valley Review Short Fiction Contest," he says, like it'll mean something to me. "Three hundred bucks," he shouts from his kitchen after he pulls the issue out of its plastic wrapping. I hear the champagne pop. "For a story?" I ask. It seems impossible, but he's nodding when he comes back through the doorway. His face is flushed, thick auburn hair a mess from the way his hand always pushes through it. His blue eyes gleam. I step closer to him, drawn into his orbit. He's like Jupiter, I think, or whichever planet has those glittering rings of dust. They circle eternally, never flying free, held by a powerful orbit.

He scoops one arm around my waist and taps his glass against mine so they clink. Bubbles float up from the bottom of our glasses. In the liquor store he pressed a hundred-dollar bill onto the counter and winked at the cashier, who only gave him a five and three quarters in change. I sip it slowly, rolling the sweet sparkle around in my mouth. "Can I read it?" I ask, after I swallow, a sudden tartness stinging my throat. He pauses, purses his lips. His eyes settle on the wooden bookshelf my uncle made me for Christmas the year I turned fifteen, which I gave to Jonathan for his birthday back in March. "Sure," he says. "Yes. Of course."

THE STORY ISN'T what I expect. It's set in Bracebridge, not Hixon River, and the protagonist, the main character, is a guy, a draft dodger nicknamed Trout.

Still, halfway through, there's the scene from Josie's wedding.

He describes it like I told him, with only a few altered details. Instead of the community room at the arena with a Pee Wee practice down on the ice, the wedding is in a former cannery turned into a banquet hall. There's roast beef and red fingerlings drying out in the chafing dishes, when Josie had turkey and mashed potatoes. The same fake lilac bouquets in clear glass vases with blue ribbons around the thick plastic stems. Lara, who Jonathan's never met, was on her fifth glass of table wine and already hammered. Up at the mic she unfolded her speech, then crumpled it up in a ball and told the eighty-six people in the room how Bruce first fucked Sam—although she didn't use that word, she said *seduced*, I remember, although I don't remember what word I used with Jonathan—back when they were only fifteen. In a mildewed tent trailer set up behind his uncle's barn, a detail Jonathan retained.

I'M NOT SURE how to feel when I read the story. Robbed, I suppose. Like part of me, a page from my diary, from all our diaries, has been shown to everyone on earth.

"How—" I start, but he cuts me off.

"It's fiction," he says, voice firm.

I shake my head. I've spent enough time with him to know that writing isn't like coring stone and hefting it out intact. "It's about the gemstones," he told me once. The lecture given in bed, his palm sliding up my bare hip. "You take what you want from the grey shatter of life," he whispered, then rolled over and snapped on the light to write the line down.

HOURS AFTER LARA'S speech, when we were all good and wasted, Josie kept saying, "It's fine, it's fine," like she was the only one who'd been hurt. We were outside, Lara on her back on the grassy median pointing out the constellations as if we hadn't all learned them at the same time, on the Grade 7 Mackenzie Island trip. While glaring at Lara, Sam wiped at the cake crumbs caught in the sequins on Josie's dress. My eyes stung from tears that might have been genuine or might have been faked. It seemed all right as we edged past the rage, all that sputtering emotion, but I could sense the encroaching cold, and in the last photo taken of us, Sam and I are squished in the middle, Josie on one end, Lara beside me, the lake a blank blue page behind us. We were eighteen, and that was the final rupture. The clearest dividing line we could imagine between childhood and becoming adult.

In Jonathan's story, the women fight, but they take it offstage while Trout does shots at the fake luau bar with his best man, bemoaning his lost lifestyle. He doesn't deal with the conflict between us, and I know it's because he doesn't understand, not really. Jonathan always wants to hear stories like the one about Bradley Dunlop, who tried to hydroplane over an open hole in the ice and didn't make it, or Arnie Belair, who dropped acid before he went hunting with his buddies and died from a gunshot wound, or how we jumped off the cliffs on Lake Matinenda every July, plunging until our toes touched the underwater city of sunken logs. He is a man, so I suppose the drama of female relationships—how deep they run, how rocky—just doesn't appeal. He wants action, adventure. Conflict. Climax.

"What if Josie sees it?" I ask, the journal hanging from my hand. "Or Lara or Sam?"

He laughs and says, "They won't." He licks the sticky champagne off his lips, presses them together so his mouth turns into a thin line. "If I'd known it would bother you..." he says.

I want to tap my finger against the black letters on the page, marching so steadily in even, explanatory lines, and say, *This is mine. This is* ours.

You cocksucker, I'd add. *You asshole.*

But I don't.

Instead, I lift the story up to cover my face and finish reading. Trout and his new bride walk a path in the woods for photos, passing through the mist off a waterfall that tumbles into a crumbling gorge. He drapes his jacket around her shoulders while the family watches, framed by the wide doorway of the old cannery. Later, he fumbles a clichéd kiss with a bridesmaid in the kitchen, his hand cupping her ass through the thin yellow taffeta of her dress while the catering staff moves around them, oblivious, and the bridesmaid, overweight, with a flush of acne on her chin, kisses him greedily back.

"Oh, shit," I say out loud, the magazine's spine hitting hard against my knee. My mouth tastes sour. "I think that's it," I tell him. "I think we're done."

"Because of a story?" he says, surprised.

I don't hear it as a question, although it might be one. He doesn't speak as I go around his place stuffing items into my purse—a loose sock, the box of tampons from under the sink. While I search out every personal fragment, I remember the night Josie and I told him about her wedding. More and more details spouted out of me, as Josie faked laughter at our old selves and tried at first to get me to stop. Her free hand heavy on my arm as I plunged forward, thinking all the while how none of it actually meant anything, how no one else would ever care so much, as much as us.

That night, on Josie's back deck, Jonathan manned the barbecue while we stood with drinks in our hands, poured into red plastic glasses. Josie's cheeks burned; there was an embarrassed smirk on her face as I talked, and Jonathan gazed at her, assessing her like she was an essay he was marking up with careful red ticks.

I could tell that part of her was pleased to be the centre of attention, so I kept going right to the bitter end, right to the precipice, nearly tipping into that truth about Bruce: his hand on my ass in the dark hallway outside the washrooms, the saccharine taste of his lips, this secret like the hard nut of a tumour that grows as you age, finally too big to be easily cut away.

Instead, I stopped myself and said, "And now he's gone. Good riddance."

I lifted my cup as Josie shot me a startled look, blinked her way back into the moment.

"Fun while it lasted, huh, Jose?" I said meanly, poking a finger into the extra flesh on her waist, watching her coy grin disappear. Jealous, I suppose, of how Jonathan had been looking at her, as if she was so exotic, had lived such an interesting life.

Acknowledgements

THANKS TO YOU, Reader, to Winnipeg's Millennium Library (especially Danielle Pilon) for my Writer-in-Residence position in 2020-21, and to my agent, Sam Haywood, for her tireless work for my books; Book*hug's Jay and Hazel Millar and Charlene Chow, for sensitive, attentive reading, and undertaking the labour to lovingly guide so many great books into the world (I'm honoured to be among them); designer Ingrid Paulson, for creating a gorgeous cover that speaks volumes; editor Meg Storey, for enriching the book with eagle-eyed attention to repetitions and insightful notes on structure, language, characterization. The epigraph is a quotation from the novel *Transatlantic* by Colum McCann.

THANKS, ALSO, to the editors and publishers who gave earlier versions of these stories their first homes in literary journals and anthologies: *Prairie Fire* ("Triple Feature," "Zombies," and "Rhubarb," which won the 2013 fiction prize, judged by Mike Barnes), *The Fiddlehead* ("Bones"), *Little Fiction* ("Places Like These"), *The Dalhousie Review* ("Point of Ignition"), *Taddle Creek* ("The Great and Powerful"), *The New Quarterly* ("That Lift of Flight" and "Empty Nest"), *The Puritan* ("Extraordinary Things"), *Descant* ("Home Wrecker," published as "Ghost Story"), and *This Magazine* ("Stories"). "Culture Shock" appeared in *Bluffs: Northeastern Ontario Stories from the Edge* (ed. Laurence Steven, Your Scrivener Press). "Rhubarb" was selected by editor John Metcalf for publication in *15: Best Canadian Stories* (Oberon Press).

THANK YOU to all the writers I know and love, including those within the vast and rich Manitoba community (Ariel, Donna, Angeline, Charlene, Conni, and so many others...) and the WriteRamble group. I'm also indebted to Julie Intepe for her long friendship and the original tale of the rhubarb liberation operation, and Erna Buffie for reading through several drafts of these stories and offering her impressions and astute notes. My mother, Laura Carter, has also read and given feedback over the decades, and I am forever grateful for her artistic eye, wisdom, love (to the moon and back), as I am for the steadfast support of my sister, Carey (thanks to both of them, as well, for being up for that odd and interesting trip to Lily Dale that mutated into the title story of this collection). Finally, to my husband, Jason: thank you for your love, wisdom, curiosity, support, and sense of humour, which keep me rooted, ready for adventure, and aspiring to continue reflecting this life in art.

About the Author

LAUREN CARTER is the author of four previous books of fiction and poetry, including *This Has Nothing to Do with You*, winner of the 2020 Margaret Laurence Award for Fiction. She has also received the John Hirsch Award for Most Promising Manitoba Writer. Her debut novel, *Swarm*, was longlisted for CBC's Canada Reads. Carter's stories and poems have been published widely in journals and longlisted multiple times for the CBC Literary Prizes. Her short story "Rhubarb" won the *Prairie Fire* Fiction Award and was subsequently included in *Best Canadian Stories* in 2015. She holds an MFA in Creative Writing from the University of Guelph. An Ontarian transplanted to Manitoba in 2013, Carter lives on Treaty One territory, within the homeland of the Métis Nation, just outside of Winnipeg, where she writes, teaches writing, and mentors other writers. She writes regularly about her creative process at www.laurencarter.ca.

Colophon

Manufactured as the first edition of
Places Like These
in the spring of 2023 by Book*hug Press

Edited for the press by Meg Storey
Copy-edited by Stuart Ross
Proofread by Charlene Chow
Type + design by Ingrid Paulson
Cover image ©Shemelina/iStockPhoto

Printed in Canada

bookhugpress.ca